Unspoken

Brenda Rothert

Chapter 1

Palmer

I grinned at the image of the bride in the magazine I held, picturing her classic, beaded veil and big cascading curls on myself.

"You like?" I asked, turning the magazine around for my design partner Georges to see.

"Eh," he said, frowning. "Maybe if you were going to prom in 1985. Add some pink frosted lipstick and dark blue eye shadow."

I narrowed my eyes at him. "I don't want my hair pulled back tight the way you like. Brady wouldn't like it either. He likes to touch my hair. You know, run his hands through it."

Georges gave me a horrified stare. "Not on your wedding day, Palmer! What about the photos? Tell him to keep his caveman hands to himself until the wedding night."

Just the words *wedding night* brought on a tingle of excitement. Not that Brady didn't bring it every time we had sex, but the idea of wedding night sex was especially hot. He'd told me about a fantasy involving his face between my thighs while I still had the dress on, and I couldn't deny that I was now fantasizing about it too.

"We still have quite a few details to work out," Georges said, looking up from the bridal magazine he was flipping through to give me a chastising look over the dark rims of his glasses.

"I know," I said, snapping out of my sexy reverie about Brady. "Let me get out my wedding planner."

"Let's finish this over sushi," Georges said. "I skipped lunch and I'm starving."

I glanced down at my watch and shook my head. "Ugh, it's after six. I can't. My mom asked me to stop by her house on my way home, and I told her I'd be there around six."

"Damn you. Now I have to get carryout." Georges rolled his eyes dramatically.

"I'll buy lunch tomorrow," I said. "Don't forget that we're going to the florist's shop for a dry run of the centerpieces."

Georges' face brightened. "Let's go visit the dress again too."

"Maybe," I said, smiling at him. "It has been a full week since we last saw it. I'll see you in the morning, okay?"

He nodded and turned back to the magazine. I checked my phone on the way to the parking deck, smiling when I saw a message from Brady.

Brady: Going to see Dad. Be home late. Lunch tomorrow? Love you.

I wrote back, glancing up occasionally to make sure I didn't crash into anyone.

Me: Lunch with G tomorrow. I'll cook dinner tomorrow night at my place. Love you too.

We still called it my place even though he'd practically moved in. Once married, we planned to live in my tiny bungalow instead of his tiny apartment. Between Brady's building skills and my design ones, we'd made my place into a cozy love nest.

On the drive to Mom's, I let my mind wander to the job I'd just been hired for. I was designing a nursery for twins – a boy and a girl. My client loved a traditional look, so I was using gingham, soft yellows and greens and gorgeous white painted furniture.

This job was creating unexpectedly strong maternal pangs. Brady and I both wanted kids, but we wanted to wait a couple of years. He was paying a price for his father's lousy decisions, and we both had to focus on our careers for a while.

Still, I let myself dream about the day we'd have a baby. Hopefully one with his dark hair and bright green eyes.

I parked in front of Mom's house, noticing the faded maroon shutter that had been hanging by one screw had finally fallen off. Brady had offered to paint the dingy brownish exterior when Mom and Danny moved in here last year, but Mom always put him off, saying she knew he was too busy with work.

This place needed a spruce-up, though, even if Brady and I had to show up and just do it. Weeds were beginning to overtake the small flower bed next to the front porch.

When I pulled open the creaky back screen door, Mom glanced up from the kitchen table and stood, meeting me for a hug. She held on longer than usual, and I studied her face when she pulled away.

"You okay?" I asked.

"Yeah." She headed for the stove, not meeting my curious gaze. "I made you a plate of dinner. Chicken pot pie."

I sank into a chair at the table, looking around the kitchen for my younger brother. "Where's Danny?"

On cue, his wheelchair came rolling into the room.

"Almer!" he cried, reaching out his arms. I grinned and stood, bending down to hug him tight, the way he liked.

As soon as I released him, he turned his chair around, grunting with the effort, and worked his way back out of the room.

"Where are you going?" I called behind him. "I just got here!"

"Cubs," he said shortly.

I smiled at his retreating form, realizing I should've guessed from his baseball hat and Cubs t-shirt that he was immersed in a game on TV. Though he was twenty-three, Danny's doctors said he had the mental capacity of a four-year-old. But I knew he was smarter than they gave him credit for. No matter what his mental capacity, he was the brightest ray of sunshine in my life. I'd been in one fist fight in my life – when I was eight and a kid in our neighborhood called my five-year-old brother stupid.

Mom set a plate down in front of me, fussing over grabbing the salt and pepper shakers and a napkin and pouring me a glass of iced tea.

"I can get that stuff. Sit down," I said. "This looks delish."

"How are the wedding plans coming?" she asked, her eyes warming with excitement.

"Good. I'm going to make the final decisions on the flowers tomorrow."

I blew on a steaming forkful of pot pie, studying my mom's drawn expression. She didn't bother with fixing her hair or makeup, since she spent her days taking care of Danny. But the lines on her face were more pronounced than usual. Something was off.

"What's up?" I lowered my fork and set it on the plate. "You look worried."

She sighed deeply. "It's probably nothing."

"What's probably nothing?"

"I got a call from the hospital today about the pre-op testing for my back surgery."

"That's right," I said, chiding myself for forgetting to call her about it yesterday. "Is there a problem with the surgery?"

Hopefully the doctor hadn't changed his mind about it helping her, or the insurance hadn't denied coverage. Mom needed this surgery. Years of lifting Danny in and out of his chair had left her back aching every minute of the day, though she rarely complained about it.

"They did an x-ray and it showed a possible mass," she said, wrapping her arms around herself. "In one of my lungs."

My heart pounded as her words sank in. "A ..." I cleared my throat. "A possible mass? What does that mean?"

She sighed again. "It means I have to get a CT scan tomorrow. Aunt Claire came over to be with Danny while I was at the hospital yesterday, and it's an hour drive for her. I didn't want to ask her to come back tomorrow. Is there any way you could come over in the morning, around 9:30?"

"Of course." Emotions swirled inside me. This was so unexpected that I was still trying to wrap my mind around it. "But I want to go with you. I'll ask Brady to come stay with Danny."

She shook her head. "I don't know that they'll do anything but the scan tomorrow, Palmer. The results may take time. I can handle it on my own. If you'll be with Danny, that'd be perfect."

"Sure," I said, not sure at all. "Are you okay?"

She nodded and attempted a smile. "It's probably nothing. Just a precaution. They haven't cancelled my surgery or anything."

I nodded too, trying to see that as a positive indication. But the worry that had kicked up my heart rate and drained my appetite in an instant was still there.

Flowers, cake and the perfect wedding hairstyle suddenly felt like ridiculous things to care about. All that mattered right now was my mom being okay. She had to be.

Brady

Seeing my dad in an orange jumpsuit stamped with black numbers got to me even more than the handcuffs. Here, he wasn't Tucker Grant, successful contractor and businessman – he was Inmate R14738.

I couldn't feel sorry for him. He'd swindled his own clients and employees out of more than $300,000. But prison was one place I never thought I'd set foot in, and I sure as hell hadn't expected to be visiting my own father here.

He nodded over at me, bending his elbows and raising his hands in the air so a guard could unlock the handcuffs. Once free, he approached and grinned, sitting down on the other side of a table in the state prison visiting room.

"Brady," he said in greeting.

"Hey, Dad. How's it going?"

He shrugged, appearing unconcerned. "Been doing lots of reading." With a glance at the door, he realized I was alone. "Where's your brother?"

I shook my head. "Hell if I know. Hasn't shown up for work since Tuesday."

Dad's dark, silver-streaked hair was a little longer than it'd been when he started his sentence a month ago. I couldn't help wondering what the past four weeks had been like for him, but I didn't care enough to ask.

"So how's business? You keeping things afloat?" He leaned back and crossed his arms over his chest, studying me seriously.

"Are you fuckin' serious?" I shook my head. "Business is … I don't know, *destroyed* might be a good word for it. You know clients started dropping us right and left when you got indicted."

6

A shadow crossed his face. "That's part of the job. You have to get those clients back or replace them with new ones."

"Yeah, ones who don't watch the news," I muttered.

He pointed a finger at me and spoke in a low, ominous tone that would've scared the shit out of me several months ago. "Watch it, you ungrateful prick."

"Or what?" I shrugged carelessly. "You left me a huge fucking mess to clean up, do you realize that? I've had to lay more than half the guys off. I went through my entire savings trying to keep the business open when we've got no work. No one trusts Grant Builders anymore, and it's your fault."

He snarled and gave me a dismissive wave. "Piss on that. The only one in here is me, so don't act like you're paying any sort of price."

"You let the entire company down." I held his gaze, making sure he heard me. I'd wanted to say these things for a long time. Months. Since the day he'd been taken away from a worksite by two detectives. I'd known from the time I heard the charges read in court that he was guilty. I could see it on his face. He'd kept business accounts I never knew about, which added to the betrayal.

"You don't see your old man for a month and you come here to bust my balls?" He arched his brows at me. "Come on, tell me what's new with you. How's my future daughter-in-law?"

I sighed deeply, willing my blood pressure to go down. "Palmer's good."

"When's the wedding?"

I shrugged and looked away. "Supposed to be in five weeks."

"What's that mean – 'supposed to be'?" His brow furrowed with concern.

I unclenched my jaw to respond. "Well, like I said, I've gone through my entire savings. I'm supposed to be paying for the wedding."

"That girl of yours deserves the best."

His admonishing tone made me want to fly across the table and shove him to the floor. Didn't he realize I wouldn't be in this situation if not for his reckless greed?

"Yeah, I agree," I said bitterly. "But like I said, I'm broke."

"So scale back. It doesn't mean you can't get married."

"Palmer's spent a lot of time planning this." I rubbed my forehead, my stressful financial situation rising back up to the front of my mind. "I don't want to have to tell her we can't do any of it. I already had to postpone the honeymoon."

Dad cleared his throat and looked from side to side. Apparently deciding no one was listening, he spoke in a low tone. "Listen, I've got an account you can access. One the cops never found."

My face twisted with disbelief. "Are you fuckin' kidding me? You think I'd take a dime of your dirty money?"

He narrowed his eyes at me. "You want your wedding or not?"

"Not like that, no." My muscles tensed with nervous energy as anger rose inside me. "See, this right here is what you've left me with. Every fucking body – even you, apparently – thinks that because you're a dishonest cheat, I must be, too. But I'm not. I'm breaking my fuckin' back trying to save the business, but it's sure as shit not for you. It's for all the people who need their jobs there."

He gave a disgusted grunt. "Have it your way. But I need you to access the account and get some money to an attorney for me."

"Fuck you."

"Dammit, Brady," he said, leaning forward in an effort to intimidate me. "How many times have I come through for you? I put you through college, taught you most of what you know about building houses and gave you a great job at my company. All I need is for you to facilitate a transaction. I just need you to get my money to an attorney for my appeal."

"Facilitate this," I said, flipping him off. "It's not your money."

"I can't believe I raised such a goody two-shoes," he muttered.

"I can't believe my father's a thief." I stood from the chair. "Great to see you, Dad."

I turned and nodded at the guard next to the door, who opened it for me. Why had I come here? I knew him well enough to know he wouldn't be sorry. But I'd still wanted to tell him to his face about the damage he'd left in the wake of his spending spree.

Resentment boiled inside me as I made my way through the many doors of the prison, each of which had to be unlocked by guards entering codes into keypads. Two months ago, I'd thought it was all smooth sailing from here. I was making decent money and was about to settle down with a woman who was everything I'd ever wanted and more. But the rug had been pulled out from beneath me. Nothing made sense anymore.

I'd waited to propose to Palmer until I knew I could give her the wedding she deserved and have enough money to start our life together. My newfound money problems didn't just keep me up at night with worry, they also made me feel undeserving of her.

I turned the key in my pickup truck and it roared to life, throwing up gravel as I drove away from the prison. No matter how far I got from my father, I'd never be able to break away from his reputation.

Palmer

The scent of sautéed garlic and the cool, sweet taste of Moscato took the edge off of my tension. But when Brady walked in the front door, the rest of my worries drained away. I met him halfway, my open arms telling him what I needed better than words could.

"Hi, baby," he said in my ear. He'd pulled my body against his, lifting my feet from the floor. I wrapped myself around him, clinging for dear life.

"I'm so happy to see you," I said, taking in his sweaty, cedar scent. The solid strength of him filled me with warmth and relief.

I didn't want to let go when he lowered me to the ground and leaned back to look at me.

"You okay?" he asked, his green eyes filled with concern. "How'd it go for your mom with the test?"

"We don't know yet." I reached up to his face, running my fingertips over his black stubble and then higher, stroking them through his short hair.

"Dinner smells amazing," he said, looking over at the stove.

"You smell amazing." I pressed myself back into his chest and he mumbled an approving grunt, bending to kiss me. I pulled his lower lip between my teeth, letting him know I wanted more than a sweet hello kiss.

His arms tightened around my waist and he picked me back up, carrying me toward the bedroom.

"You missed me last night," he said, a smile in his tone as he spoke against my lips.

"I did." I moaned with satisfaction as he kissed my neck, going right for the sweet spot beneath my ear.

When he lowered me to the bed, I unbuttoned the jeans I'd changed into after work, tugging them down. He grabbed the waistband and finished the job for me, pulling my panties off with them. He raised up my t-shirt and lowered his lips to my stomach, kissing it lightly. I writhed beneath him, loving the build-up and wanting more at the same time.

The tickle of his stubble across my skin set me on fire. I gripped his shoulders and ran my fingers through his hair. There wasn't room for worry now. My desire consumed me, a powerful rush that forced all other sensations and thoughts aside.

Brady pulled my shirt off, his fingers deftly unfastening my bra and casting it to the floor. And then, he just looked. This undid me every time he did it. Sometimes he'd undress me completely, leaving all his clothes on, and just stare at my body.

My chest rose and fell as I panted. His eyes had darkened with desire, and I wanted him now. But Brady was enjoying himself too much to give in just yet. He stroked a hand over the large bulge in his jeans, his gaze washing up and down my body.

When he ran his fingertips over my breasts lightly, I couldn't help crying out. My body was humming with desire, and his slight touch only stoked my desire for more.

"Spread your legs," he murmured softly. When I slid my thighs apart, he groaned and tightened his grip on his bulge. I reached over and pushed his hand away, replacing it with my own.

"You see what you do to me?" he said, meeting my eyes. "Just looking at you. You're so beautiful, Palmer. And all mine."

He ran a fingertip down my stomach, continuing down to my clit, which made my body tense up as I cried out his name.

"God, that feels good," I said breathlessly.

A small smile played on Brady's lips as he stripped off his t-shirt. The sculpted muscles of his chest and arms were bronzed from outdoor construction work. I pulled my knees apart further as he unbuttoned his jeans and they dropped to the floor. His boxers were next, and then he was climbing onto the bed, all dark, muscled perfection, and I closed my eyes and arched my back.

He kissed my thighs, but apparently decided he'd teased me enough then. When he filled me with one thrust, I wrapped my legs around his waist, knowing I wouldn't last very long.

There was nothing between us now. We'd stopped using condoms when we got engaged, deciding the pill was enough. That had changed things emotionally more than I'd ever expected. The joining of our bodies was almost spiritual now – the way we connected before he left a part of himself in me.

He knew my body well, and he responded to my tensing muscles by moving faster, harder – exactly what I wanted.

His breath was hot against my neck, and I pulled his hair, on the edge of the blissful release only he could give me.

"I love you so much, Palmer," he said softly, pressing his lips to my neck. And that was it. I shattered into a million pieces, the sensation heightening to a level I could hardly bear when he thrust into me one last time and groaned against my skin.

We both relaxed our bodies, lost in a cloudy haze of contentment.

"I've been wanting that all day," I said, smiling as he pulled my body against him.

"Damn, that was hot." He arched a brow at me. "I need a picture of you, all spread out like that."

I felt my cheeks darkening at the thought. What was sexy in the moment now made me self-conscious. "Why take a picture when you can have the real thing anytime?"

He leaned up on an elbow, looking down at me. "I have to take a job out of town. You know things are bad, and I've got no choice if I want to keep the guys working."

"Of course. Do what you need to do."

"We have to leave tomorrow. The job's in Iowa. We'll probably be three weeks. I hate to leave you now, with the wedding so close and all. We're gonna work six tens, but I'll be home Sundays."

"Go," I said emphatically. "Please go, and don't worry."

He brushed the hair back from my face and wrapped a hand around my neck.

"How was it with your dad?" I asked. "I know you texted that it was fine, but …"

Brady flipped onto his back and sighed. "I shouldn't have gone. The asshole's not sorry, which is no surprise."

"Oh, shit!" I cried, jumping out of bed. "I forgot to turn off the stove!"

I ran for the kitchen, the smell of burnt garlic hitting before I was out of the bedroom. Switching off the burner, I moved the skillet of blackened garlic to another burner. When I walked back into the bedroom, Brady was pulling on his jeans.

"Let's go get pizza," he said. "I can't stay tonight. I have to find Troy so I can drag his ass to Iowa in the morning."

"You and your brother couldn't be any more different," I said, searching the floor for my clothes.

"One of the guys told me he got kicked out of his apartment for not paying rent. So if I don't take him with me, he'll take up at my place while I'm gone. It'll be full of beer cans and whores when I get home."

"No whores allowed in my future husband's apartment," I said, hoping to lighten his mood.

"They've got nothing on you anyway, baby," Brady said. He ran a hand through his hair, his expression clouding. "I'm sorry things have been shit lately with me. My dad and my brother and work. And cancelling the honeymoon."

13

"We can go another time," I said, waving a hand dismissively. "Keeping your business going is more important."

"I'll make it up to you," he said, his expression serious as he met my eyes.

"Brady, it's not a big deal." I stopped to pull my shirt on, unable to have such a serious conversation in only a bra. "The timing isn't right, and I completely understand."

His face tightened with disappointment, but he nodded. "I know. I just never imagined being in this situation. I waited until I could take care of you to propose. And now it's all going to shit."

I reached up to his broad shoulders, where my hands met rock hard tension.

"We're gonna be okay," I said. He nodded again, but was it doubt that flickered across his face? I had an unsettled feeling myself, but surely that was just from stress. When things calmed down, everything would feel right again.

Chapter 2

Brady

Sweat rolled down my face, a couple of drops ending up in one of my eyes. I pulled my t-shirt over my head in a quick motion, using it to mop my face off.

"It's six," Hunter said, poking his head up over a peak in the massive roof we were shingling. "We quittin' or keepin' on?"

I shrugged and pulled a nail from between my teeth so I could speak. "They're paying double time for Sunday. Might as well do another hour."

There was a low grumble of disappointment from the guys, but they wouldn't be bitching when they got paid. Everyone was sour from not getting to go home today, but this made more sense. It was a five-hour trip home to Chicago, one way, and we were here to make money. At the end of this three weeks, I planned to give them all several days off to rest.

I'd have a few days to spend with Palmer before our wedding. Even though we'd scaled back on things to save money, she was more excited than ever. This job had come at a great time – it would pay for our entire reception dinner. I hated going to bed in a fleabag motel here alone every night, but it would be worth it to see the smile on her face as she walked down the aisle toward me. I wanted to be the man who came through for her, even when it seemed impossible.

I glanced at my younger brother, who'd been glued to my side from the second we arrived here. He was dragging ass, probably from the forced detox. I wouldn't let him have so much as a beer with dinner. Moderation wasn't Troy's strong suit, and damned if I'd let him end up in jail like our dad. He was a screw-up, but he was still my brother.

"You good?" I asked in a stern tone. He nodded and got back to work.

His suffering would be for nothing when we got home and he fell back in with his deadbeat friends. Here, I could control his every move, but there, I couldn't.

From my vantage point on the roof, I had a perfect view of the muted orange shades made by the sun's nightly retreat. The sunset here provided a perfect backdrop to the endless stretches of dark green corn stalks. This place was peaceful – a far cry from the congestion of big city life.

Palmer would love the sunsets here. That thought rang through my mind at the end of every work day. I was missing her bad, especially since I hadn't made it home today.

The guys were silent as we closed out the work day, drained from a twelve hour day in the sun. We packed up our tools and everyone headed out for dinner. I sent Troy with Hunter and drove back to our motel, pushing the button on my console to call Palmer as soon as I started the truck engine.

"I miss you," she said as soon as she answered, a smile in her warm tone. I smiled, too, picturing her wearing shorts while sitting in her favorite chair, her long legs inviting me to run my palms up underneath those shorts.

"I miss you, too."

"You sound tired," she said. "Long day?"

"Yeah. And I'm supposed to have your legs wrapped around my waist right now, so there's that."

Her laugh had a hint of arousal in it, and my cock stirred in my jeans at the sound of her voice. "Mmm. That sounds so good, Brady."

"It's gorgeous here, baby. Quiet. I think you'd like it."

"Yeah? Maybe we can stay at a bed and breakfast there sometime."

I'd been planning to wait until I got home to broach something with her, but I tossed it out now on an impulse.

"How do you feel about Colorado?"

"Um, I feel good about it, I suppose. Why? You want to take a trip there first?"

I took a deep breath, going for it. "I wanna move there." There was silence on the other end of the line, so I decided to make my case. "The construction market's good there. And I wouldn't have the stigma of my dad's reputation to battle. I've decided to release my interest in his business and start one of my own. Damned if I'm gonna work my ass off building his company back up while he's in prison."

"That makes sense," she said. "Starting your own business. You have a lot of business savvy."

I shrugged. "What I don't know, I'll have to learn. But I've got to have a new market. And I need to get Troy the fuck away from Chicago. He's got potential, but he has to be kept away from temptation."

"I just … what you're saying makes sense, but I've got my family and business here."

I'd thought of her potential objections, and was prepared.

"Can't we bring them with us? I'll be able to help with the cost. I've been asked to bid on a huge hunting lodge near Denver, and I'm pretty sure I'll get the job."

"Brady." She sighed softly, and I wished I'd waited to have this conversation face to face. "My mom ... she has to get a biopsy."

"Shit. I'm sorry, baby. Why didn't you call me?" I pulled into a gravel parking lot, throwing my truck into park so I could give her my full attention.

"We just found out Friday, and I figured we could talk about it when you get home. There's definitely a mass, but the doctor doesn't know if it's cancer or not."

"Is she doing okay?" I rubbed my forehead, wishing I was there with her. Fuck double time. Palmer was upset, and I was in another state.

"She seems okay. But she doesn't want to upset Danny, so I'm not sure how she really feels. She's just acting like nothing's happening."

"What about you?"

"I'm trying to be level-headed. I don't want to jump to the worst conclusion, you know?"

"Yeah. I'm sorry I brought up moving. If I'd known—"

She cut me off. "Brady, no. You're just being practical. You have to think about your business. There are people whose families rely on you for those jobs. I'd do the same."

"Let's just wait 'til after the wedding to talk about it," I said, trying for a soothing tone.

Palmer sighed deeply. "I've been thinking maybe we should put off the wedding."

My mouth dropped open in shock. "Put it off? You don't want to marry me?"

"Of course I do, Brady. It's just … my business isn't doing so great, either. We can't afford anything that we planned, and we need to be realistic about it."

"I'm working twelve hour days here," I said. "This job is gonna pay for our reception. We'll figure the rest out."

I waited for her to agree, gripping my steering wheel so hard my knuckles whitened.

"You've gone through your whole savings. And I can't even think about the wedding with what's going on with my mom. I want our wedding to be a happy time, not a stressful one."

I pushed a button to switch the call to my phone, opening the door to my truck and stepping out for some air. My chest was tightening over this unexpected change of heart from Palmer.

"It's because I'm broke, isn't it?" I said bitterly. "You got engaged to a man who made a good living and now I've got nothing."

"Brady, no," she said hotly. "Don't do this."

"Don't do what? React to you calling off our wedding?"

"I didn't say I want to call it off. I said we should wait, which is not the same thing."

I rubbed a hand down my face and leaned against my truck. "Fuck that, Palmer. If you wanted to marry me, we'd find a way."

There was a momentary pause before she lashed out in a way that was very unlike her. "Fuck me? Fuck *you*, Brady, for putting words in my mouth. I never said I don't want to marry you. I'm worried sick about my mom. How dare you start this with me right now?"

"How dare I?" My voice rang out in the silent rural countryside. "How dare I feel something when you cancel our goddamn wedding? I'm busting my ass here so I can spend my last dime on our wedding, and you're saying 'no thanks.'"

"I said no such thing! Stop being an asshole."

"Oh, now I'm an asshole?"

"I'm not doing this right now, Brady." Her aggravated tone made my anger boil over.

"When's a good time for you, Palmer? When would you like to decide if we're getting married in less than four weeks?"

"I don't know what's going on with my mom, and you're talking about moving to another state, and I just can't do this right now!" Her frantic tone reminded me that I never should've brought this up over the phone.

"Okay," I said in a level tone. "It's gonna be okay. I will be home next Sunday so we can talk. I'd come home right now if I could."

"I'm sorry."

Her weak, strangled tone meant she was crying. I leaned a forearm on the window of my truck, bending and pressing my forehead to my arm.

"Don't cry. I love you so goddamn much, Palmer."

"I love you, too. I want to marry you. You know I do. It's just that ... if my mom gets bad news ... and I think you're right, you should start your own business. But you need some money to do that. I don't feel right spending this money you're making on frivolous things when you need it for that."

She seemed to have decided already. A knot of tension felt like it was about to burst in my chest, but I forced myself not to get worked up again.

"Let's talk about it when I get home."

"Okay."

I heaved out a sigh and stood back up. "I have to get a shower and some dinner. I'm beat."

"Call me tomorrow?"

"Yeah. Talk to you then."

We both hung up, and I climbed back into my truck, tossing the phone on the passenger seat. I really was beat, and not just from the long day of roofing. Once again, someone I'd thought was a solid presence in my life had pulled the rug out from under me. Palmer wanted to call off our wedding.

And even if she did just want to wait, there were other things at play now. Things caused by my greedy, piece of shit father. Between the business and my efforts to manage my brother, I was rowing a sinking boat alone.

I turned toward the parking lot exit, trying to clear my head. But it was useless. Until I went home and figured things out with Palmer, I'd never have a clear head.

Palmer

Mom shook the raindrops from her umbrella, wrapped it into a tight bundle and stuck it in her giant bag.

"Quite a storm we're having," she said, running a hand through her brown shoulder-length hair. "Is it supposed to stay rainy tomorrow?"

I glanced at her and shrugged. I hadn't thought about much of anything but her health since she'd been summoned to this appointment after her biopsy.

"Dr. Fielding's office is on the second floor, want to take the elevator?" I asked.

"Sure. That'll be quicker."

I hadn't suggested it to save time. Mom had dark circles under her eyes and her clothes were baggy. At first I'd told myself she was probably worried about these biopsy results. But when I was restless and alone with my thoughts at night, I admitted the truth: she'd been looking tired and fragile for a couple months.

"I think I'll make those brownies Danny likes when we get home," she said as the elevator rose. "The ones with the marshmallows."

We stepped off and checked in at the front desk. Mom grabbed a magazine and took a seat next to me in the bright, airy waiting room.

"Palmer," she said, nudging me. "Look at this darling kitchen curtain made from dish towels. I could do that in my kitchen, couldn't I?"

Part of me wanted to ask her – kindly — to stop with the small talk. I wanted to retreat inside myself and mentally prepare for this appointment. But this was her way of coping, and her state of mind meant more than mine.

"Yeah," I said, eyeing the green and white checkered fabric. "I can help you do it. And maybe add some green accent dishes on that shelf by the window?"

She agreed, moving on in the magazine to the beef casserole dish that looked so good she needed to copy down the recipe.

I was relieved when at last we were called into an exam room – a white space with a painting of a sunset on one wall. I stayed there while Mom was led away by a nurse who wanted to check her weight and blood pressure.

It wasn't about wanting or not wanting to know if my mom was sick. I *needed* to know. Waiting for this news was brutal. The best and worst case scenarios churned through my mind during every waking moment. But even then, I considered the possibilities with a sense of numb disbelief.

A tall, bald man followed Mom back into the exam room.

"Carl Fielding," he said, shaking her hand and then mine. He took off his white coat and laid it over the back of a chair. Leaning back against a counter, he crossed his arms and met my mom's gaze.

"Janelle, the biopsy indicated that the mass is cancerous," he said, an apology in his tone.

Mom slumped in her seat, pressing a hand over her mouth. I looked from her to the doctor in a stupor. I'd told myself I was prepared for this diagnosis, but I wasn't.

"I'm just getting back surgery," Mom said, crying softly. "That's all."

"Chest x-rays often help us find this," the doctor said. "The good news is that what you have is treatable."

Mom's shoulders rose as she sat up straight. "Okay. Good. If it can be beat, I'll beat it. I have to."

The doctor's eyes softened with sympathy. "This cancer is treatable, but not curable."

"What does that mean?" she asked, pulling her brows together.

"It means we can extend your life with treatment."

"So this is going to kill me." Her face twisted with emotion. "But my son ... I have a son who needs me."

The note of pleading in her voice was like a knife to my heart. I cracked, tears flowing freely down my cheeks.

"I'll take care of Danny, Mom," I said, reaching for her hand and squeezing it. She turned to me and the quiver of her lower lip sent me into a full-on sob. This was my mom – the woman who had raised me, cared for me and loved me unconditionally. And she was hurting. It was more than I could stand.

"Tell us about the treatment," I said, wiping away my tears. I wanted to grab ahold of this situation – be the one in control so Mom could absorb the shock.

The doctor passed me a pen and notepad. "Just in case you want to write anything down," he said. "It can be tough to remember everything."

Scribing his explanations onto the lined paper was my focus. I prodded him to explain things to me in depth, because making myself understand this situation felt more manageable than allowing myself to feel it.

Mom hardly moved. She wrapped her arms around herself, and suddenly I saw her as vulnerable for the first time ever. It was sobering.

"I'd like to start treatment immediately," Dr. Fielding said. "Can I have my staff set up something next week?"

"Yes," I said.

"No." Mom turned to me, her brow furrowed. "Not with the wedding so close."

She was putting me first, even now. I wanted to scream at the unfairness of her being sick.

Not just sick, a voice in my head reminded me. *Dying. She's dying, Palmer.*

That voice would have to shut the hell up for now, because I couldn't go there.

"This is more important," I said, leaving no room for argument. Her face fell with disappointment.

"All I've ever wanted was to be a good mom," she said, her voice wavering with emotion. "And now I won't be able to take care of Danny and I'm ruining your wedding."

I scoffed and squeezed her hand. "Mom, stop that. I can't possibly think about the wedding with this happening." I turned back to the doctor. "Next week will be fine."

"Do you have any other questions for me?" he asked, resting his hands on his knees.

A foggy sense of disbelief still clouded my head as I shook it. Mom and I rose to leave the office and I grabbed her arm. Was I trying to steady her or myself? I wasn't sure it mattered. In this moment, we were clinging to each other for support.

But I realized on the elevator ride down that it couldn't stay that way. I had to be the strong one. Hopefully, the more stress I could shoulder for my mom, the less she'd feel.

I held the front door to the building open for her with a renewed sense of purpose. My mom and Danny needed me. I wasn't going to let them down.

Scratches on the dark wood of my kitchen table blurred as my vision clouded with tears. How could there be any left? I'd been crying all afternoon, and I had a throbbing headache to prove it.

Footsteps from Brady's heavy work boots made their way toward me in a steady rhythm. How many times had I asked him to take those damned boots off at the door?

"Hey, babe," he said, walking into the kitchen.

"Hey." I wiped my wet cheeks with my fingers and met his gaze.

"Bad news, I take it."

I nodded. Though I knew I could fall into his arms and cry as long as I wanted, I crossed my arms over my chest instead. Things weren't right between us. We'd just been texting – not talking — since our argument a week ago.

"Let's talk about it," he said, pulling out a chair on the other side of the table and sitting down.

I recalled the notes I'd taken during our appointment. "She has small cell lung cancer, but that's not a good thing. It's aggressive, but treatable. They'll be starting chemo right away."

"I'm so sorry. How's she doing?"

I sniffled and tried to hold back a fresh surge of tears. "Awful."

He nodded, reaching across the table. He took my hand in his big, work-worn palm, stroking a calloused thumb across my wrist. The concern etched on his face made my stomach churn.

"I can't get married right now, Brady. I couldn't even go to work Friday. My mom has a long road ahead of her, and I have to be there for her and Danny."

"I'll be there, too. I understand about putting off the wedding."

I stopped trying to suppress my tears. I didn't cry in front of Mom or Danny, and I needed to right now.

"What about Colorado?"

Brady shrugged. "I'll be fine here. I already gave up my interest in Dad's business. I'll go work for someone else."

I felt a glimmer of hope. Maybe this was going to work out after all.

"What about that big job? And the employees?" I asked.

He shook his head. "There'll be other jobs. And the employees … I can't find jobs for all of them. I wish I could."

"Some of them have worked for your dad for more than twenty years, haven't they?"

Brady nodded solemnly. "Yeah. And the worst part is that he wasn't investing the money for their retirement like he was supposed to. They've got nothing, and they don't even know it yet. I'll have to tell them when I cut 'em loose."

"What's going on with Troy?"

"He's an adult. I'll keep putting my boot in his ass, but he'll have to get his own shit together."

My heart twisted with love and sorrow for this man. He was willing to give up his chance for a fresh start as a contractor for me. What would be left of his pride, if he laid off all his employees and stayed here to be a hand on another contractor's crew, with the stigma of being Tuck Grant's son following him on every job?

And how would he feel about having to look after not just his younger brother, but mine too? Danny was a far greater responsibility than Troy.

"Go to Colorado, Brady," I said, meeting his bright emerald gaze. "Go kick ass and take names. I know you will. Take your brother and give him a fresh start, too."

He drew his hand back, his brows knitting together with concern.

"You don't want me here?" The hurt in his tone was like a slap to my face.

"It's not that. I want you here, but I don't *need* you here. I have to focus on my mom and Danny. You need to focus on your company."

"Fuck that, Palmer. No job means as much to me as you. But if I'm not needed—" He pushed his chair out and stood. "I'll fuckin' go."

"I don't want this to end badly," I said in a pleading tone.

He scoffed and glared at me. "Well, I don't want it to end at all. But here we are."

Finding out about my mom's cancer had knocked me on my ass and I was still down. And this was just another thing. A thing that wasn't life and death. A thing I just didn't have room to deal with right now.

"Is there someone else?" Brady asked bitterly.

"For fuck's sake, are you kidding me?" I slammed my hands on the table and stood. Now I was shaking, a mix of fury and sorrow pushing me to my breaking point. I took a calming breath and slid the cushion cut engagement ring from my finger, holding it out to him. He stared at me with a mixture of shock and fury.

"I don't want the motherfucking ring back," he said. "Pawn it and take your new boyfriend on vacation."

"I kind of wish I had one right now, because you're being such an asshole."

He laughed bitterly. "I thought we were forever, Palmer. And you're ripping my fuckin' guts out here. You're lying to me about something. You know if I found out who the other guy was I'd beat the living shit out of him."

"I've never been with anyone but you."

"Is that it, then?" He took a step closer, and the tall, muscled frame that had always made me feel safe suddenly became intimidating. "You want to be with other guys? You don't want to marry your first?"

"No. I don't want anyone else." I looked down at the floor.

"Is it because you weren't my first? You said that didn't bother you."

"I just think we both need some space to deal with our issues."

"Isn't that something we're supposed to do together?"

The venom in his tone flipped a switch inside me, and I looked up at him, my cheeks flaming with anger.

"You can't know what this is like," I said. "This isn't like your dad going to prison. My mom is seriously ill."

He cut in, staring me down. "This isn't supposed to be a game of who has it harder."

"I never said it was a game. You just refuse to back the hell off, and I just can't do this right now. I can't."

Instead of responding, he spun around and paced across the kitchen, his fist connecting with the wall. I jumped and gaped at the hole he'd put in it with his bare hand.

"Brady—"

He gave me a final murderous glance before turning to leave, covering the distance to my front door in a few seconds. The slam of it closing brought forth another round of tears.

I knew this was best, but it still hurt like hell. I had to give Mom and Danny my all. I was moving in with them so I could be there whenever they needed me. And even though Brady was pissed right now, I hoped that with time he'd come to see that we both needed this.

Chapter 3

Eleven months later

Brady

I ran a hand through my hair and walked into the deli where I was meeting Derek. Bits of sawdust flew from my hair onto my shirt. So much for my plan to shower before lunch with my old friend. I'd lost track of time in my workshop this morning.

The cluster of people around a booth gave away Derek's location. He'd been recognized even without a jersey identifying him as a member of Chicago's NFL team. I hadn't seen him since flying to Chicago for his engagement party last month. He was marrying an actress who was an even bigger celebrity than he was.

I approached the booth and Derek grinned at me. "There's my buddy, guys."

The small crowd of fans started clearing out.

"Hey, thanks for saying hi," Derek said to them, handing back something he'd autographed for one of them.

I shook my head as I sat down. "This is the last thing your ego needs, man."

He shrugged his broad shoulders. "Looking good, Grant. You been hitting the weights?"

"A little. Mostly it's just work."

"Aren't you the boss?" He cocked his brows at me as a waitress approached and looked at us expectantly.

"Iced tea, please," I said.

"Me too," Derek said.

The young brunette waitress gave me a shy smile before leaving the table.

"Still got it, I see," Derek quipped.

"Yeah, so do you, but you're throwing it away and getting married."

His smile reminded me of the skinny kid who'd sat down next to me in English class on the first day of eighth grade. We'd been friends from then on.

"We're thirty-two, Brady. Gotta grow up sometime. And I'd have proposed to Adriane no matter how old I was when we met. She's incredible."

I bit back a comment. His fiancée seemed like a nice girl, and she sure as hell wasn't after his money. She had plenty of her own.

"So what's new, man?" he said. "How's life in Colorado?"

"No complaints," I said, shrugging. "Work's been crazy, but that's a good thing."

"You seeing anyone?"

"No." I wrinkled my face with disgust.

"You talked to Palmer at all?"

"Fuck no. We've got nothing left to say to each other."

Derek leaned on his elbows, considering his words.

"This is probably gonna piss you off, but I think you made a mistake with her. She'd just gotten terrible news, and you flew off the handle."

I crossed my arms over my chest and glared at him. "She didn't want to marry me anymore. I couldn't help getting pissed over that. I'd have given up everything for her, but she didn't want me."

"Maybe the timing was just off. You were dealing with that shit with your dad, and she'd just found out her mom was sick. I'm just saying you should've reached out to her, at least as her friend. You haven't been the same since you guys broke up. Does it still bother you?"

I pinched the bridge of my nose and sighed. "Does it bother me? I practically got an ulcer over it. I was pissed at the whole world for months after she dumped me. I couldn't sleep. I worked sixteen hours a day and spent every weekend fucking drunk. At least I'm a functional person again now. I hope I never see Palmer again."

Derek shook his head. "You still care about her, though?"

"I'm over it. Probably dodged a bullet anyway. I'm never getting married."

"Don't bring down my wedding with your bullshit attitude, man."

I grinned. "Me? I'll be too busy entertaining the bridesmaids."

"Yeah, Adriane's got some hot friends. You'll thank me for asking you to be a groomsman."

The waitress set down our plates, meeting my eyes for a second as she grabbed my empty iced tea glass.

"I'll get you more tea," she said, flushing.

"You enjoying the single life?" Derek asked when she was out of earshot.

I shrugged. "It's a lot simpler. We fuck and I leave. None of the emotional shit."

"If it works for you, I'm happy for you. But I've never seen you happier than when you were with Palmer."

I shifted in my seat with aggravation. "Will you drop it, asshole? She dumped me a year ago. We're over. And not that it's not good to see you, but we haven't hung out in a while. Why is my famous buddy gracing me with his presence today?"

"We need to hang out more. I'm busy, but I can always make time. I want you to get to know Adri better, too."

"Yeah, that'd be good."

"I want you to build me a house," Derek said, his eyes fixed on my expression.

The waitress set my glass down and I grabbed it, thinking for a few seconds as I took a sip.

"Me?"

"Yeah, you know – your business. It's my wedding gift to Adri. She loves it here in Chicago, and I just signed a contract that'll keep me here for a while. It's a good time for us to build."

"I'm guessing we aren't talking about a shack," I said, grinning wryly.

"I want the best."

I shook my head slowly. "I don't know. I usually do million dollar homes, Derek. Not ten million dollar ones. And I'm booked. Over-booked, actually, for the rest of the year."

"Good thing we've been friends since junior high. Otherwise I'd think you were saying no."

I laughed and arched my brows at him. "Look man, I work in Colorado now. I can recommend someone who builds for famous people here."

"Fuck that." Derek waved his hand. "You're one of my best friends. I know you won't fuck me over. And you do incredible work. You've done a great job of digging out of the hole your dad left you in."

"Yeah, but—"

He cut me off. "But nothing. Just because you don't run your mouth about how successful you are, that doesn't mean I'm not aware of it. I want you building my house."

I considered my schedule. "When?"

"Now. I bought a three-acre lot in the suburbs last week."

I shook my head, adamantly this time. "There's no way. I've got all my guys booked for the next six months solid."

"Hire more, then. I'll pay. You're a closer. Always have been. I want you building my house."

I thought about it. There was nothing in my life but work now. I was finally on sure financial ground again so I didn't need the work, but I was intrigued by the challenge. And I wanted to come through for my friend of almost twenty years.

"Alright," I said, shrugging. "I'll have to work my guys extra and hire some new ones, but I'll make it work."

"Thanks, man. I need to know it's in good hands since I can't be as involved as I'd like."

"I'll build your mansion, asshole," I muttered.

"When are you gonna build one for yourself?"

I shrugged, my jaw tensing. After Palmer broke up with me, I'd burned the plans I made for our log home. It was something we'd daydreamed about together, but I'd never told her I was secretly drawing up plans. The thought of building any place for myself still stirred up memories of what I'd lost.

"I'm happy living above my office. No commute," I said.

"Women don't give you shit about it?"

I glared at him. "Women don't give me shit about anything. I don't need that noise. And women don't come there, anyway. I go to their place."

"Good," Derek said dismissively. "You live your dream and I'll live mine."

I finished my food in silence. My dream had left me a year ago. And as crushed as I'd been, now no one held any control over me. It wasn't a coincidence that I was making more money than my dad's business ever had. Work was my new passion, and it would never let me down.

Palmer

Georges stared at his reflection in the small mirror he kept at his desk. His short blond hair was as perfectly styled as it had been when he'd last looked at himself three minutes ago.

"Dammit, I should've had my brows done. I look like shit," he whined.

"Georges, the client doesn't care what you look like. She just wants to talk about our design work," I said as I typed numbers into my computer.

"But she's famous, Palmer. Like hugely famous. I've seen her movies."

"She's very down to earth."

"If you were into pop culture, you'd get it," Georges barked.

I laughed and shook my head. "Like I have time for that." I looked up from my laptop and focused on him. "Listen, seriously, don't be a star-struck idiot. We are professionals. Redesigning her office was a huge job for me, and she could recommend us to her friends."

Georges' squeal was so loud and girly that I broke out in a grin.

"I could meet my dream man!" he cried. "He might be an actor or a musician! Or, *oh my God*, the model for that new Calvin Klein thing. Do you think she knows him?"

The knock on the door of our office suite wiped the smiles off both our faces.

"Be cool," I hissed in a low whisper. "Do *not* fanboy her."

He made a pouty face at his mirror and I rolled my eyes. I walked to the door and opened it, and Adriane Hunt smiled widely at me.

"Palmer! How are you, sweetie?" She strolled in, sliding her big dark sunglasses up to rest on her head.

"I'm good." I reached out to shake her hand and she embraced me warmly instead.

"You need a spa day," she said, running a hand over my dark hair. "We should do that soon."

"That would be amazing," I said. "I could use pretty much every service officered at a spa." I gestured to Georges, who was standing at his desk. "This is my business partner Georges."

He shook her hand eagerly. "I'm a fan, Ms. Hunt."

"Why don't we sit down in the lounge?" I suggested, leading the way through the door to our casual office area. It was furnished with a couch and several comfy chairs. We'd redone it recently, giving it a clean, modern style with cream shades and pops of turquoise.

"This is gorgeous," Adriane said, waving a hand around the room.

"Thank you. This was all Georges. The style, I mean. We both painted and re-upholstered the furniture."

"So you saw in my messages that I loved the finished look of my office," Adriane said.

"I was thrilled to hear it. Since you trusted me with most of the choices, I was a little nervous," I admitted.

"I'm so glad I called you when I read that magazine article about you being the best kept design secret around. You get me,

Palmer. I can't even describe my interior design style, but you get it."

"That's a high compliment, thank you. Your style is very much like my own, which made it easier." I turned to Georges. "Her apartment is amazing, you'd love it. Tons of light. It's about twenty percent shabby and eighty percent chic."

"Nice." He nodded appreciatively.

"I'm getting rid of it, actually," Adriane said, grinning. "I'll be selling it next year because ..." She held out her hand, where a diamond ring flashed on her finger. "I'm getting married!"

Georges squealed and she grinned at him.

"I know!" she cried. "He's such a doll! A dream. We're building a house together."

"How did I not hear you were engaged?" Georges asked, his brow furrowed.

"We've managed to keep it quiet. We had a tiny engagement party – only about 20 people. My publicist and his are working on an announcement right now. So now I can wear my ring outside the house."

"It's spectacular," Georges said, admiring the ring up close. "Who's the lucky guy?"

"You'll know soon," Adriane said breezily. "So about the house we're building ... I want you to do the design work." She turned to me and smiled broadly. "Please tell me you can work me in. Please."

The room filled with silence. I looked at Georges, who was biting his lip hopefully.

"Adriane, we'd be honored," I said. "But you should know that Sinclair Brammer Design is a young company. We've never done anything on the scale I imagine your home will be. It's just Georges and me."

She waved her hand and stood. "I have complete confidence. You worked a miracle on my office and I can see from this room that Georges has just as much talent. I have to head to New York soon and I'll be completely immersed in filming. I want you guys to make every decision on this house. Give it the modern, feminine touches you're so good at."

"Of course," I said, my heart pounding over this opportunity.

"This will be a big house," she said. "Around 18,000 square feet, I think. The architect is finishing the plans now."

"We won't let you down," I said, watching as she pulled her long blonde hair into a ponytail.

"You've got my cell," she said. "I'll take you to the lot soon so you can get to work with the contractor."

"Who is the general contractor?" I asked, pulling out a notebook to take notes.

"I don't know his name. He's a friend of my fiancé. I'll text soon, okay, sweetie? I have lunch with my agent, I'm sorry."

I stood and she hugged me. When Georges stood, she embraced him too, and his face glowed with happiness.

"Let's try to fit in a spa day before I go to New York, Palmer," Adriane said. "You look worn out."

"I am," I admitted.

"I'm really excited about this, guys," she said as she headed for the office door. We said our goodbyes, and as soon as the office door closed, Georges slapped a hand over his mouth to suppress his squeal.

"Holy shit!" he whispered in an excited tone. "Did that just happen?"

"I think so." I let the excitement flood me. I needed this. I *was* worn out, and this project would help energize me. Georges and I had dreamed of a break like this.

"Oh, it's almost two thirty," Georges said, glancing at his wristwatch. "Didn't you need to take your mom to the doctor?"

"Yeah, thanks for reminding me."

"Wanna Skype about this tonight?" he asked excitedly.

"Definitely. As soon as I get Danny to bed, I'll text you."

I was sketching plans in my mind as I walked to my car. Though I didn't know what the floor plan would be, it was easy to let my imagination run wild. I was eager to dive in to this project. It was also a welcome distraction from the dread that had settled in my chest. I'd been trying to focus on anything but this appointment, but there was no putting it off anymore. I had to get my mind in the right place on the drive to my mom's house.

Dr. Fielding's face said it all: the corners of his mouth were turned down and his eyes were soft with concern. He reached for Mom's hand and patted it.

"I'm sorry, Janelle. The cancer isn't responding to treatment at this point."

Mom sighed, her bony shoulders dropping with disappointment.

"I figured," she said softly. "I knew all along it was only treatable and not curable. But still ..."

She stopped, wiping the corners of her eyes and breathing deeply. I forced my own tears back. Not now. She needed me to be strong and supportive, and I wouldn't let her down. But inside, my heart had just shattered into a thousand pieces.

"What are our options?" I asked the doctor, clearing my throat. I wrapped an arm around Mom's shoulders, wishing I could infuse her with comfort.

"We need to discuss your wishes for the end of your life," the doctor said, taking care to address my mom and not me. I liked that about him – he never let her feel like she was being talked about like she wasn't even here.

She squeezed her eyes shut and pressed a hand over her mouth. I wanted so badly to cry with her. This was about as un-fucking fair as it got. A woman who had sacrificed so much didn't deserve to wage a losing battle against a disease that was eating her body away slowly, stripping her of her strength.

"Danny," she choked out, her eyes in agony as they met mine. "I'm not upset for myself, it's—"

"Mom," I said, turning to meet her tortured gaze. "I will never let Danny down. Ever. I'll be with him every step of the way. Please don't worry about him."

I turned to the doctor and offered an explanation. "My younger brother. He's disabled. Mom is his caregiver."

He nodded a bit, the cruelty of this scenario seeming to set in with him, too.

"You've talked to me about him, Janelle. There's counseling available for all three of you that may help ease your concerns."

"I've taken care of him since he was born!" Mom burst into fresh tears. "I'm the only one who's ever taken care of him. Palmer's been helping this past year, but … I knew this would happen, but …" She gave the doctor an apologetic glance. "I'm sorry. You have other patients. Let's get back on track."

The doctor took off his glasses, a sad smile turning up the corners of his lips. He was a trim, balding man with a fatherly concern etched on his clean-shaven face.

"We are on track, Janelle. This is what I'm here for. It's very understandable that you're concerned about your son's future right now." He turned to me. "Is there other family we can bring into the mix to discuss Danny's care during the duration of the illness and afterward?"

The duration of the illness. My mother's death was clinical to him – it had to be. But his words made me feel like I'd just been kicked in the stomach. My mom was dying. We'd known since the diagnosis nearly a year ago that she was terminally ill, but treatment had helped us deny it. Now it was staring us in the face: ugly, shadowed masses displayed on an x-ray sheet behind the doctor.

"My aunt and uncle have been helping one night a week when we need it. Like after chemo, when she's really sick."

"Good."

"I don't want my brother to be responsible for Danny," Mom said softly. "He's been telling me to put him in a home for years."

"I'll be responsible for Danny, Mom," I said. "I want to take care of him. But if I need to be with you at the hospital, Kevin and Dana will take good care of him."

Mom shook her head, a bitter expression distorting her fragile, lean face.

"I never wanted to burden you with this, Palmer," she said.

"It's not a burden. I love Danny. We're a family, Mom."

She reached for my hand and squeezed her bony fingers against mine.

"Okay," she said, meeting Dr. Fielding's gaze. "No more treatments, then. How long?"

"I can't say with certainty," the doctor said. "But I think within three months."

Mom nodded slowly. "Okay. I'll have to start thinking about how to tell Danny."

"I'm here for anything you need." Dr. Fielding put his glasses back on and looked from Mom to me. "Call anytime, okay?"

"Thanks." Mom smiled weakly and the doctor laid a hand on her shoulder. He turned toward the door and I spoke without even thinking. I needed a mission – an assignment. Something I could control. The vagueness of this situation was making my chest constrict.

"Wait. What happens now? Is she going to be in pain? I don't … I mean, what should we do? Is she going into the hospital?"

"Not at this time," Dr. Fielding said. "If she's in pain or having problems, that's when you should call me. I recommend counseling and hospice services. It helps to get your fears out in the open, even if there isn't a solution for all of them."

"And she'll still see you?"

"Yes. I'll see her again in two weeks." He looked between us again, checking to see if we had more questions.

I had so many. What will I do without my mom? How can I help Danny understand? Is she going to suffer?

But Dr. Fielding couldn't answer those questions. No one could. Like I had so many times over the course of the past year, I had to dig deep and find the strength my mom needed me to have right now. Danny would need me, too. I'd thought a year ago that I'd be coming up on my first wedding anniversary right about now. Instead I was trying to figure out how to cope with the deepest sadness I'd ever known.

Chapter 4

Brady

The blonde a few barstools down from me locked her eyes on mine as she slid an ice cube from her glass and ran it across her lips. A drop of water slipped past her lower lip and her tongue snaked out to catch it.

"Hey," Derek said, waving a hand in front of my face. He turned to see what I was looking at and shook his head. "Sorry, was I interrupting your moment?"

"No." I tipped up my glass and finished my beer. "What were you saying?"

"We were talking about that shit beer we used to drink in high school. Tasted like jet fuel."

"Yeah, but we all pretended to love it," I reminded him, laughing.

"Life was so simple back then. Just playing football and chasing girls."

"Isn't that still your life?" I arched my brows with amusement.

"There's pressure from contracts and sponsors now," Derek said. "It's not just for love of the game anymore."

"I know. You've got a lot of eyes on you. It can't be easy."

"That's one of the reasons Adri's so good for me. She lives a high-profile life, too. She doesn't resent me for it."

The blonde was leaning toward the bar now, her eyes still on me. She was pretending to adjust her low-cut top, but really she just wanted me to see her touching her tits. And they were nice ones, but ...

Like always, my mind wandered to the one place I didn't want it to. Palmer. Her tits were perfect B cups, with round pink nipples I'd never been able to get enough of. I'd loved unclasping her bra and sliding it off her shoulders to uncover her tight nipples. Tasting them, touching them, watching them bounce when she was riding me ... damn, did I miss her body.

That image brought on a barrage of unwelcome memories. Palmer breathing hard against my neck when she was about to come. Winding her soft, sweet legs around my waist. Saying she loved me. Locking those dark chocolate eyes on mine.

"Either go get her number or ask her to blow you in the alley," Derek mumbled, shaking his head. "This is bullshit."

He thought I was focused on the blonde, and I wasn't saying any different. I grinned at him and motioned to the bartender for another round.

"Sorry, you're used to being the center of attention these days, aren't you? Want me to beg for your autograph? Will that make you feel better?"

"Fuck you," he said, shaking his head and laughing. "Seriously, if you were alone, would you be getting on that right now? She's been drooling at you since we sat down."

I glanced at the blonde and shrugged. "Maybe. She's okay."

"Not really your type," Derek said under his breath, nodding this thanks when the bartender sat two more beers in front of us.

"Oh yeah? What's my type?"

"Brunette." He furrowed his brow, considering. "Slightly thinner than her. Pretty smile. Named Palmer, maybe?"

I scoffed and reached for the fresh beer, taking a long drink. "Not anymore. Like I told you, I like it easy these days, man. I'm never getting my ass dragged into a relationship again."

Derek gave me a skeptical look, but I decided not to push it. It didn't matter whether or not he believed me.

There were plenty of women out there who wanted the same thing I did. And none of them would infiltrate my mind the way Palmer had. I resented the hell out of still thinking of her. She'd moved on almost a year ago. I had too, but I wondered if the memories would ever get the message and go the fuck away.

Palmer

Adriane flashed her perfect white smile at me as she handed over a cup of hot coffee in a carryout cup.

"You look tired, sweetie," she said. "Drink up."

"Thank you." I sipped the black coffee gratefully. After taking a day off yesterday to be with Mom and Danny, I hoped working today would be good for me. I needed to get started on plans for Adriane's house.

I'd been stretched so emotionally thin in the past couple days that I crashed for nine full hours last night as soon as I got Danny to bed. I'd put ice packs on my eyes when I laid down to help with the swelling from crying. When I looked at my reflection in the mirror this morning, I thought I'd looked better than I had in a while.

"Do I look bad?" I asked Adriane, feeling self-conscious.

"Not at all, you're gorgeous," she said with a laugh.

"No, I mean when you said I look tired."

She sighed and took a sip of her own coffee. "Don't we all in the morning? I was up way too late last night watching a movie."

I tried to remember the last movie I'd seen. The only one I came up with was a horror movie I'd seen with Brady at a theater more than a year ago. Now life provided all the horror I could handle and then some.

"So it's just back in here," Adriane said, slowing her sports car and narrowing her eyes to search. She eased onto a dirt road that led into a secluded, wooded area.

"This is beautiful," I murmured. "It's right on the edge of the neighborhood but completely private."

"We're serious about our privacy," she said. "The photographers hound us. Our security people are putting in an alarm system and cameras. You'll have to sign a non-disclosure agreement and get a security pass to go on the property. I'm sorry, but it's required."

"I understand. It's no problem."

She grinned at me and put the car in park. I surveyed the large area that had been cleared of trees. The basement was already dug, and a couple dozen construction workers were busy with different jobs.

"I love this, Adriane," I said, stepping out of the car and closing the door.

"Me too!" Her enthusiasm was contagious. She grabbed my arm and led me closer to the work site.

"It's going to be brick, with a horseshoe drive. And a huge pool and guesthouse. Oh, Palmer, this is our contractor—"

"Brady," I finished, my pulse pounding. At the sound of his name, he turned our way and I nearly lost my footing, though I was standing on flat ground.

His expression remained impassive, but a storm raged in his bright green eyes. His jaw tensed as he studied me, and I reminded myself to breathe in and out.

Those broad shoulders and chiseled biceps were so familiar. I'd gripped those shoulders for dear life when he made love to me for the first time, sure I'd drown in the flood of emotion. Those lips had traced every inch of my body, and I'd run my hands through that soft, short black hair more times than I could count.

I knew this man better than anyone, but time had stretched a wide divide between us. A divide I'd created. The distance between us had expanded so much over the past year that I didn't know him anymore. What was he thinking as he stared at me? Did he miss me as much as I missed him? I couldn't tell. Not anymore.

"What the fuck is this?" he demanded, turning his gaze to Adriane. Her brow furrowed in confusion as she looked from him to me and back again.

"I'm wondering the same thing," I said. "Why aren't you in Colorado?"

"Palmer?" Adriane said. "What's going on?"

"I ... we know each other," I explained.

"*Used* to know each other," Brady corrected tersely.

"We used to be involved." My tone was soft as I dropped my gaze to the ground, unable to stand the tension radiating from Brady.

When I looked up, he was handing the papers in his hand to the man next to him. He walked over to us, glowering at me every step of the way. As he got closer, Adriane backed up a step. She was probably intimidated by the tall, broad man who was clearly pissed at one or both of us.

"Engaged," he said, his tone cold. "We were engaged, Palmer. Or have you forgotten?"

I commanded my chin to remain level. I was a professional, and this was a job. "Of course I haven't forgotten."

"What are you doing here?" he demanded.

I held up the dark leather bag I carried design plans in. "Working."

"Working?" He glared at Adriane.

"Shit," she muttered.

"Yeah." Brady crossed his arms and looked from her to me.

"Didn't my fiancé tell you we'd be using the designer who did my office reno?" Adriane crossed her arms. She was regaining herself now.

"Yeah, but he failed to mention it was Palmer. Probably because he knew I wouldn't have taken the job." Brady was pissed, and a sense of disappointment began building in me. I was going to lose this job, which I badly needed.

"Does he know you two were involved?" Adriane arched her brows at him in challenge.

"Hell yeah he knows. He was supposed to be a groomsman in the wedding."

"Derek?" I said, my stomach sinking even further. "You're engaged to Derek?"

Adriane held up her hands in a calming gesture. "Listen, surely we can all be—"

"God dammit!" Brady shook his head with disgust. "Fucking Derek. I already moved shit around so I could be the foreman here."

"Look, I should be the one to leave," I said, looking at Adriane. "I can recommend another designer, or Georges can do the field work."

Adriane shook her head. "I want *you*, Palmer. I have to be in New York filming for the next couple of months, and I need to know you're involved in this house every step of the way."

"Brady's work is much more important than mine," I said. "He'll make sure your house is perfect. Maybe I can come in at the end and help you furnish it."

Adriane glared at Brady. "Isn't Derek giving you a blank check for this project?"

Brady's face darkened in a scowl. "What the fuck is that supposed to mean?"

"This house is his wedding gift to me. It's going to be our dream home. He wants you to build it because he says you're the best, and I respect that. But I want Palmer doing the design work. Are you saying you refuse to work with her? Is that what several million dollars buys us? A childish fit from our contractor?"

Silence hung, and I half expected one of the guys in the background to make a quip along the lines of 'Oh, *burn*.' I was digging my nails into my palms, my heart pounding. Apparently Adriane didn't know how few people had ever put Brady Grant in his place.

He sighed deeply. "Fine. I'll work with her. But tell Derek his ass is mine when I see him again."

My muscles slackened with relief. I wasn't losing the biggest job I'd ever been offered.

"Brady, I'll make myself as scarce as possible," I said, hoping to smooth over the tension. "I'll make this as painless as I can."

He scoffed and rubbed his dark, unshaven jaw line. "Painless? You? I won't hold my breath."

Agitation sparked my defenses. "I'm a professional. As long as you are too, we won't have any problems."

"What do you need from me at this point?" he asked in an aggravated tone.

"I'll need to go over the plans with you."

"Can it wait an hour? I need to get my guys started on something."

Now his tone was resigned, which was almost worse than the anger. His emerald gaze made my heart pound, and I took a deep breath to steady myself.

"It doesn't need to be right now," I said. "We can do it tomorrow."

He nodded. "I'll be here at seven, but after nine would be best."

"Okay. See you then."

He turned and walked away silently, and Adriane gave me a sympathetic glance.

"He's rather intense," she murmured.

"Yeah."

"Really hot, too."

I turned to her, my heart fluttering at her assessment of him.

"Don't tell Derek I said that," she said, pointing a finger at me. "How tall is he?"

"Brady? Six foot three."

"He's all muscle, too. Does he actually do the building work, or does he just supervise?"

I tried not to look his way. "He does both. He's a perfectionist. And Brady's very hands-on."

"Bet you miss having those hands on you." Adriane was studying Brady's backside like a wildcat eyeing its next meal.

"Hey." I snapped my fingers to bring her attention back to me. "Remember your hot, rich fiancé who's building this mega-house for you?"

"Oh, I'm madly in love with Derek," she said, grinning. "And for the record, I was rich before we got engaged. I'd never mess around on him. But a girl can still look, you know? And appreciate a hot man when she sees one."

"Well, I need to get back to the office if that's okay."

"Sure," Adriane turned, leading the way back to her sports car. "And I'm going to meet Derek for lunch. I'll have to remember to warn him that his ass is Brady Grant's."

I smiled and followed her.

"Can I ask why *your ass* isn't his anymore?" she asked over her shoulder. "He obviously wanted to marry you. Why'd you break up with him?"

I hiked the strap of my heavy bag up on my shoulder. "It's complicated," I said.

"Hmm," she said dismissively. "Well, he is a bit of a hothead, but still, seems like your loss."

"It was," I agreed, glancing over my shoulder at Brady's form. "It definitely was."

When I walked into my office, a dark green takeout cup from my favorite coffee shop was waiting on the edge of my desk. I didn't even have to ask what it was. Georges knew me well. Better than anyone else did these days.

"Apple Pie Frappuccino," I said, sighing happily. "Georges, you don't know how much I need this right now."

"You sounded stressed," he said, not looking up from the drawing he was focused on creating at his desk.

"We haven't talked since yesterday."

I sank into my leather office chair, setting down my bags and grabbing the cup of liquid relief from my desk.

"In your text," he said absentmindedly.

I wrinkled my brow and turned to him. "All I said was '*On my way*'. How did you get that I was stressed from that message?"

He leaned down to the drawing, squinting at a detail. "What are you stressed about?"

"Seriously, tell me how you knew."

He sighed, looking up from the desk to glare at me over the dark, thick rims of his glasses.

"You were going to the site of the biggest job we've ever been offered. You've been giddy about it for days. Normally you'd be calling me before you were out of the driveway to tell me about it."

"Hmm." I took a sip of the Frappuccino and closed my eyes, savoring the apple cinnamon flavor.

"Palmer." George's tone conveyed his annoyance. "What happened? Is it about the job?"

I sighed and met his serious gaze. "Sort of. Not exactly. The general on the house is Brady."

"Oh, shit," Georges said softly, covering his mouth with his hand to hide his smile.

"Yeah, laugh it up," I muttered.

"Well, maybe you won't actually have to see him."

"I saw him this morning."

Georges' brows shot up with interest. "How does he look?"

I glared at him and set my cup on my desk. "Pretty much the same."

"Tall, dark and sexy?" Georges' dreamy tone made me roll my eyes.

"It'll be fine." I unloaded papers from my bag onto my desk and flipped open my laptop. "He'll be busy, I'll be busy and our work won't overlap that much."

"That was the first time you've seen him since … you know. Was it weird?"

"Yeah, a lot."

I opened my billing program, eager for a distraction. I hadn't been able to think of anything but Brady since the moment I'd seen him this morning. He looked good. Even better than I remembered, if that was possible. His hair was a little shorter, but I liked it.

His sharp tone and the anger in his eyes had thrown me. It was like no time had passed since our breakup. The pain of losing him had dulled some for me over the past year. I no longer remembered his cedar scent on my bed sheets or the warm sensation of his lips on my skin.

But the hurt was still fresh. Not just for him, but for me, too. I'd never imagined my life without him once we got engaged. But in the span of just a few hours, everything changed. Mom's diagnosis had sealed an unexpected future not just for her, but for me, too. My future was now wound inextricably with my brother's.

"Did you send out the Sullivan invoice?" I asked Georges, scanning my electronic file.

"Did it Friday."

I clicked out of the program, starting a new file on Derek and Adriane's house. This was truly a dream assignment for me and Georges. We'd never done a new build on such a grand scale. The budget was pretty much unlimited. I was anxious to dive in, but with a glance at my watch, I realized I'd have to wait until tonight and start the plans at home.

"I have to leave for the day," I said to Georges. "Do you need anything from me?"

"No."

"I'm meeting Brady tomorrow to go over the plans for the new job. Do you want to meet me there or should I pick you up here?"

Georges looked at me over the rim of his glasses again.

"Do you want me to do it?"

I sighed, considering. "No. I think it's best that we get the awkwardness out of the way up front."

"I'll leave it to you, then," Georges said. "If I go, I'll just be staring at his biceps the entire time anyway."

I nodded and waved half-heartedly as I pulled open the door to my office. What I'd said to Georges was partially true. I did want to get past this awkwardness with Brady. But the main reason I was going tomorrow was to see him again. It had been so long – almost a year. And even though he was still angry with me, seeing him angry was better than not seeing him at all.

Chapter 5

Palmer

My brother's deep giggle sounded from around the corner, and I suppressed a grin. Danny loved scaring me, and I always played along.

He gave a monster's roar and wheeled himself around the corner toward me. I jumped and squealed, dropping my bag to the floor in pretend alarm. He broke out in a fit of laughter and I joined in. It was impossible to be in a bad mood around Danny.

"You got me," I said, bending down to meet his hazel-eyed gaze. "How are you?"

"Good." He grinned at me. "Let's walk."

"We'll go for a walk after dinner, okay? Where's Mom?"

"Right here," she answered from a recliner just a dozen feet from me and Danny. She was tucked into an afghan, so small and silent I hadn't even noticed her.

"How are you?" I asked, walking over to her.

"Pretty good. I fell asleep for a bit. How was work?"

I groaned and sank onto the couch. "Interesting. The general contractor on the house we're doing the design work for is Brady."

"Brady!" Danny yelled, looking at the front door with his brows arched in anticipation.

"No, sweetie, he's not coming over," I said gently.

"Wow." Mom sat up taller in the recliner. "Brady. It's been almost a year. How is he? Did you guys talk?"

"Just a little."

"Did he …" Mom paused. "Was it good to see him?"

I shrugged. "I don't know. He's still mad at me, and it's gonna make things awkward."

"He's mad because you broke his heart," she said. "I still don't understand why you broke up with him. You shouldn't have stopped living your life just because I'm sick."

I rubbed my forehead, frustrated. We'd been over this so many times in the months after I broke it off with Brady, and eventually it had passed. Now I wished I hadn't told Mom about seeing him again.

"Go see Brady!" Danny called. "Play baseball!"

The dark stubble that matched his hair made my brother look like an average twenty-three-year-old man. But in his mind, he was a little boy. And he still remembered playing softball with Brady. I remembered it, too. During one at-bat in every game, Brady would wheel Danny out to the first base line and park his chair near the plate. When Brady hit the ball, he'd push Danny around the bases. The first time, I'd cried. Danny's look of pure happiness as the wind whipped his hair while circling the bases had reached straight into my heart.

"I'll cook dinner," I said, getting up from the couch. "And then we can go for a walk, Danny."

He gave the grunt that signified agreement and reached for the wheels of his chair. He could wheel himself, but it was slow-going.

I loved him for always wanting to do it anyway. Danny was strong-willed and independent in his own way.

When I walked into the small kitchen, instinct made me glance at the schedule I'd posted on the side of the refrigerator. In previous months, it was a rainbow of color-coded appointments: green for the oncologist, orange for chemo, purple for radiation and yellow for times I'd need help from my aunt and uncle.

But now the stark white boxes reminded me there was nothing left to do in the fight against Mom's lung cancer. It would take her, while I watched helplessly from the sidelines.

I forced a smile at my brother. I'd gotten ahead of myself. Sadness and helplessness were only allowed after 9 pm, when Danny and Mom were settled in bed. I usually worked for a couple hours after that, before crashing in my twin bed here. That was when I allowed the darkness to swallow me. Fortunately I was usually too tired for it to last very long.

Hopefully this would be a smooth evening. Mom wasn't sick from her treatments anymore, so as long as Danny didn't have a meltdown, it would be peaceful. I was on auto pilot already, distracted by thoughts of seeing Brady tomorrow. The sight of him this morning had stirred feelings in me that had been buried for a long time – almost a year. I couldn't help wondering if I stirred any feelings in him besides anger.

Brady

I nodded to myself as I surveyed the progress on Derek and Adriane's house. The guys had worked 'til dark last night finishing grading on the lot. I'd been at another job site, but it looked like Hunter had taken care of business here without me.

Today we'd start pouring the massive basement. It was gonna be another very long day. I needed to make notes for a meeting I was having this afternoon with the architect, but I couldn't focus.

I hadn't been able to think about anything but Palmer since yesterday morning. Usually she wandered into my mind unexpectedly, but after being face to face with her, she was constantly in my thoughts.

Again, I pushed those thoughts away. I'd wasted so much time on her. I couldn't let myself get drawn in again. She didn't want me anymore, and I'd moved on.

The guys started showing up just before eight, all heading to work without much direction. I'd finally built a good crew, and they knew me well. I didn't put up with fucking around and drinking coffee for half an hour at the start of the work day. If someone didn't pull their weight, I cut them loose to keep everyone else from having to pick up the slack.

"Mornin'," Hunter said, nodding at me. I nodded back and briefed him on my plans for the day. Hunter was the one employee I trusted to lead any job in my absence. He was reserved, but he knew his shit.

This project was about to consume all my daylight time, and I welcomed it. Framing the walls of a house always got me going, so I knew starting to see a house this size come together would be a good feeling. I buried myself in directing the guys and monitoring their progress, keeping one eye on the dirt road that led to the work site.

I recognized Palmer's old Mazda as soon as she pulled up. She still hadn't bought a better car. Did that mean her business was in trouble? Hopefully not. She was good at what she did.

She stepped out of the car and I let myself glance at her. Beautiful as ever. She wore a dark skirt and a red sleeveless top with black heels, one of which wobbled as she navigated the dirt road. I looked away, fighting the urge to approach her and take her hand to steady her. She didn't want me holding her hand anymore.

"Hey," she said, only meeting my gaze for a second. Probably because I'd been such a dick to her yesterday.

"Hey," I said, holding out a set of house plans for her. "That's yours. We're pouring this morning. Should be framing in about a week. Let me know if you have any questions."

She nodded and tucked the plans under her arm. "How have you been? It's good to see you."

"I'm good."

This was where I was supposed to ask her how she was, but fuck that. I didn't want to hear about her new life without me. She glanced toward the machinery roaring to life on the other side of the lot.

My mind raced with all the things I wanted to say to her. I miss you. I still think about you constantly. Fuck you.

"You're thinner," I said.

"Yeah."

"You didn't need to lose any weight. You've always looked good."

The corners of her mouth turned up in a small smile, but she didn't look my way.

"It wasn't something I planned. It just happened. Stuff piles up and I get so busy and eating is last on the list."

"How's business?"

She shrugged again. "It's okay. We needed this job, so I appreciate you letting me stay."

I nodded and crossed my arms across my chest. I'd done something that made her happy. It made me feel like a hero and a dumbass at the same time. This woman had shredded me, and I'd have to see her on a regular basis now.

"You're welcome on site anytime," I said. "Wear boots or tennis shoes and a hard hat. All change orders go through me. And if you need to discuss anything ..." I reached into my wallet for a business card, holding it out.

She glanced down at the wording and looked up at me. Damn, I'd missed those eyes. They were hazel – an unpredictable swirl of gold, green and brown that took on different shades depending on her mood. When she was happy, they were gold. More brown when she was upset. And when she was turned on, they darkened to a deep chocolate that I still saw in dreams, however unwelcome they were.

"I still have your ... well, is your cell number still the same?" Her cheeks pinked as she studied me. "Or is it not okay for me to use that?"

I pulled the card back. "My number's the same. And you can use it if you need anything and can't find me here. Or look for Hunter, he's the foreman when I'm not here."

"Okay."

After a few seconds of silence, I decided I'd done enough to smooth things over after yesterday. "I need to go. Let me know if you've got questions on those plans."

Or if you want to tell me why the fuck you stopped loving me, I wanted to add. It was all I could do not to ask if there'd been another guy, and if she was still with him. None of our mutual friends had heard of anyone, but wondering ate at me.

Maybe the whole thing was my fault, for thinking we were happy. I had been, and I felt like an asshole for not realizing she wasn't.

"Thanks, Brady," Palmer said softly. There was no gold in her eyes today. Just the soft brown that meant something was off. This was awkward as shit, but not because she was crazy happy with her new life and had to see the ex again. It was the opposite, actually. She looked like a woman who was about to drown in her own sadness. The dark circles under her eyes stood out beneath her makeup. And still, I wasn't a worthy life preserver. Apparently going under sounded better to her than reaching for me.

I walked away, forcing myself not to say anything. We were over. Palmer was my past, and I didn't want to dredge that shit up again. Hopefully she had someone new in her life who cared that she was hurting. And if not, well, that was her own fucking fault.

Palmer

I walked in the back door to Mom's house, her mail in my hand, but the letters fell away when I saw Mom on the floor. My heart pounded as I lunged toward her tiny body, hunched over in front of the sink.

"Mom?" I set my hands on her shoulders and saw that she was gathering up shards of a broken plate. My sickening worry started to dissipate when I saw that she was okay.

"I dropped it," she said softly. Water ran onto the kitchen floor from the dishcloth she clutched in the hand that wasn't picking up the mess.

She'd always been so strong and capable, raising Danny and me alone. I didn't know how to navigate this shift – how to graciously ease her transition to helplessness.

"Hey. Come on," I urged. "I'll get this. Let's get you up off the floor."

I took the dishcloth from her hands and tossed it in the sink. She grabbed both of my arms and tried to pull herself up, but her body only wavered a little. I wrapped my arms around her and eased her up, supporting her with an arm around her waist. With her setting our slow pace, we made our way to the living room, where I eased her onto the couch.

Danny watched from his wheelchair, a frown of concern on his face.

"How's my favorite brother?" I asked, ruffling his hair. His gaze remained fixed on Mom. "Listen, I'll make some dinner. How about hot dogs?"

"Yeah," Danny said, a grin stretching across his face. Hot dogs were his favorite.

I needed to talk to Mom about not doing housework anymore, but not in front of Danny. I didn't want to upset him further. She wanted to keep doing the things she'd always done, but she just didn't have the strength anymore. Cancer was like a hardy weed – taking her life in a slow, underhanded way. We'd cut back the weed with treatment, but it was back full-force now, reminding us how cruel and inescapable it was for my mother.

Her eyes were already closed when I tucked a blanket around her and wheeled Danny into the kitchen. I turned the small TV on the counter to the sports channel he liked.

"Did you have a good day?" I asked him.

"Yeah," he said happily.

I poured a glass of milk and helped him drink half of it while I waited for the water to boil for the hot dogs. My heart sank as I realized Mom was exhausted but hadn't wanted to leave Danny until I was home to take care of him. It was time to hire some help. I couldn't really afford it, but that was the story of my life. I'd make it work.

After Danny and I had hot dogs and chips, I cleaned up the kitchen and helped him into the bathtub for a bath. I'd taken over his bath time from Mom not too long ago. Danny was heavy, and even though he was able to move some on his own and help, there was no way Mom could do this anymore.

I scrolled through emails on my phone while I sat next to the bathtub. I'd started leaving work at 4:30 when Mom was diagnosed so I could be here to help with dinner. I'd had to leave even earlier sometimes when she was getting chemo since it made her so sick. Georges had picked up my slack and never said a word about it. I always worked a couple more hours after I got Danny to bed, but I was never caught up.

A giggle from Danny made me look up from the email I was typing on my phone. He'd given himself a bubble bath beard – one of his favorite bath time activities.

"You, too," he said, grinning. I set my phone down and we worked together on a bubble bath beard for me. It must've been a good one, because he couldn't stop laughing.

Mom had always taken time for fun and games with Danny, but now that she had so little energy, he spent a lot of time watching TV during the day. I got out some hair gel and spiked his dark hair into a Mohawk, taking a picture on my phone to show him.

His laughter was contagious, and soon we were dueling it out with water guns. Though I'd forced my light mood for his benefit, I was now actually feeling a little better.

When his fingertips were wrinkled, he held them up to show me. That was our sign that it was time to wash up and be finished. I shampooed his hair and then we worked together to get him out of the tub.

I dried him, dressed him in his favorite plaid pajamas and helped him back into his wheelchair. Then we sat on the front porch together, drinking lemonade and people watching. When it started getting dark, we went inside, where I read him several stories and helped him into bed. I turned on the CD of nature sounds he loved and pulled the door halfway closed, heading to the living room to check on Mom. She was still curled up asleep on the couch, so I tiptoed downstairs.

Mom had a small two bedroom house, but I had a bed and desk set up in her basement. It had a low ceiling and '70s carpet, but I was grateful for a space of my own since I spent six nights a week here.

I turned on the baby monitor I used to keep an ear on things upstairs and settled into the chair in front of my desk. With a deep breath, I turned on my tablet and dialed Georges for a Skype session.

"Hey, gorgeous," he said, greeting me from the wingback chair he'd salvaged from a curb and re-upholstered in a beautiful purple leather. It was now displayed proudly in the living room of his small but chic apartment.

"Georges," I said with a sigh. "How are you?"

"I just did Pilates and showered, and I'm ready to brainstorm."

"Okay. Should we start with Adriane's house?"

"Sounds good to me."

We swapped thoughts and screen shots of furniture and fabric inspirations until a little after eleven, when I couldn't keep myself from yawning.

"Wanna call it a night?" Georges asked.

"Yeah. We got a lot done."

"Hey, how'd it go today with Big Sexy?"

He hadn't used his nickname for Brady since before we'd broken up. But then again, the topic of him had been off limits for a very long time.

"Pretty awkward. He said I look thinner."

"You are. Even your boobs are smaller than they used to be. Don't lose any more weight."

"It wasn't on purpose, Georges."

"I know. You have a lot on your plate, which means you ... don't have a lot on your plate." He snorted at his lame joke. "Did he say anything else?"

"No."

"Do you still miss him?"

"No," I snapped. "I'm in survival mode. A love life is not an option."

"You should talk to him. He deserves to know why you broke up with him."

My annoyance, aggravated by fatigue, was immediate. "Don't start this again. You know I told him."

"Not really. You were honest about wanting him to put his business first, but you said you were never straight about your brother."

"*Georges.*" I sighed deeply. "If I'd told him I have to move my brother in with me, he would've agreed and offered to help."

The beat of silence on the other end of the line reminded me of all the times Georges and I had gone rounds over the subject of Brady.

"It's not fair to put that on him," I continued. "He wouldn't have been able to start a business here. He would've been working for someone else and helping take care of my brother. I never would've known if he would've chosen that life or if he felt obligated to me."

"He wanted to be obligated to you, Palmer. It's why he put a huge-ass diamond on your finger. You know he and I have had our share of disagreements, but he loved you with everything in him."

"I know, alright?" My voice wavered. "I loved him the same way. That's why I didn't want to do this to him. I don't even feel human some days, Georges. I wake up, work, take care of my family, cry and sleep. That's my life. My mom is dying. Danny doesn't understand. This is so fucking hard. I have nothing left for a husband, truly. It just wasn't meant to be."

I was crying now, and since I'd broken down, I couldn't seem to stop.

"My mom was on the floor when I got home today because she broke a plate trying to wash the dishes. She could barely get up. And Danny's just so innocent and sweet that it makes me rage to think about what my mom dying will do to him. There's not enough of me. I need to hire help, but I can't afford it."

"Deep breath," Georges said in a soothing tone. "It's gonna be okay. Take a leave from work if you need to."

"I can't afford it," I mumbled, wiping away my tears.

"We're partners, and that means *partners*. I can keep up with the workload and we'll split the money like always."

"I love you," I said with a sigh. "You're such a good friend. I'll manage to find the money. This job on Adriane's house couldn't come at a better time."

"Very true. Sleep now, sweetie. Tomorrow's a new day."

I murmured my agreement and we said goodnight. I slipped out of my work clothes and into shorts and a t-shirt and crawled into bed. I could wash off today's makeup in the shower tomorrow morning. All I could think about right now was my only escape from reality – sleep.

Chapter 6

Palmer

I flipped to the back of my sketch pad and checked the basement dimensions of Derek and Adriane's house. It was monstrously huge, and my challenge was to break it up into intimate spaces that were functional and didn't feel like they were in a basement.

An image of the wine room had popped into my mind this morning before I was fully awake and out of bed. I'd showered, dressed and come straight to the work site to sketch. I always felt more infused with ideas when I was at the home site.

I had another couple of hours to work here before the appointment I'd made at a home health care place. I was hoping one of their employees would be a good fit to help Mom and Danny while I was at work during the day. It would take a load off my shoulders to know someone was there.

Brady yelled out a command to the operator of a grading machine, pointing to the other side of the lot. I glanced up from my sketch pad, but my quick look at him turned into a full stare.

His t-shirt was hanging from his back pocket. He'd stripped it away an hour ago. It was going to be another tropical, hundred-degree July day in the Chicago area. I'd pulled my hair up as soon as it was dry, and was now hiding behind my giant sunglasses.

Hopefully the glasses were allowing me to ogle Brady without him noticing. *Damn*, he was hotter than ever. The definition in his biceps, abs and back was highlighted by the sweat glistening on his golden, tanned body. He wore jeans and a baseball hat with the Grant Brothers Builders logo on it.

My gaze wandered down his body to his muddy work boots. I'd always been annoyed by the dried dirt clumps that often trailed behind him, but now … I shook my head and looked down. Now I'd give anything to hear those boots come through the front door of the small house I'd hardly lived in since our split.

I wished with every ounce of my being that he would glance over at me. Just once. Just for a second. But nothing. Being around Brady wasn't the hard part – the fact that he didn't even notice me was.

"Doing alright?"

I looked up to find Hunter, Brady's foreman, grinning down at me, hands on his hips.

"Yeah," I said, smiling back. "Just doing my sketching thing. Let me know if I'm in the way."

"Naw, you're good. We can find you a shady spot if you want, you know. You can go in our work trailer if you want to cool off. There's a bathroom in there."

I shook my head. "I'm alright."

He nodded, taking off his hat and putting it back on. He'd taken a step away from me when I blurted out a question without even thinking about it.

"How's Brady?"

He turned back to me and I felt my cheeks warming with embarrassment.

"He's okay. Works all the time. He's not seeing anyone that I know of, if that's what you mean."

I cringed. "No, I shouldn't have even asked. I'm sorry."

"You guys were engaged, right?"

"Yes."

Hunter shrugged. "He's better now. After you guys broke up, he was pissed off for a couple months. But it got better eventually. You didn't hear that from me, though, okay? I just work for him."

I nodded, wishing I'd kept my mouth shut. What if Hunter told Brady I'd asked about him? He could go tell him right now and they'd share a laugh over it.

I gathered up my stuff, my desire to flee the scene overpowering. But I had work to do. I untied my hair so it would shield my face while I sketched. Brady was managing to ignore me quite well, and I could do the same.

Brady

Derek flashed his golden boy grin when he saw me from across the bar, but I flipped him off in response. He stopped to sign an autograph before making his way to the tall table I sat at with my arms folded.

"Hey, nice scowl, asshole," he said, sitting down. "Haven't you vented enough about this by text?"

"Not even close."

"Look, it wasn't a setup. I wanted you to build the house. When Adri wanted to redo her office right after we started dating, she saw an article about Palmer and I told her I knew Palmer and she does good work. She loved her and wanted her to do the house, too."

A waitress came over and took our order, but I jumped Derek's ass again as soon as she was out of earshot.

"You should've told me, motherfucker. I hadn't seen her since the day we broke up. Do you have any idea what it was like to see her walking onto my jobsite?"

Derek leaned his forearms on the table and looked me square in the eye. "No, what was it like?"

I shook my head. "Like getting sucker-punched. I couldn't breathe for a few seconds. It was like that."

"How's she look?"

I furrowed my brow in a dirty look. "What do you care, asshole?"

"I saw her when she was doing Adri's office and she looked really overworked. We asked her to have dinner with us a couple times but she said no. I got a weird vibe from her, like something's not right."

I stared back at Derek, my heart pounding like a mallet in my chest. "You mean like she's sick? I thought she looked tired and thin, but I didn't even think …" I rubbed the stubble on my jaw and sighed.

"I don't know," Derek said. "I was just concerned about her."

"Now I can't be pissed off at you, because I'm worried about her," I muttered. He was right. She did seem off. I'd told myself she seemed different because we didn't know each other anymore, but that had probably just been the asshole in me.

I caught Derek up on the progress of the house and shoveled my burger in as soon as the waitress delivered it.

"I hafta go," I said, still chewing my last bite as I rose from the table.

"Already?" Derek's expression wrinkled with confusion.

"Yeah, I gotta get back to work."

"I'll come by to check the place out later," he said. I nodded and reached for my wallet, but he waved me off. I grunted my thanks and headed for the door.

Palmer had been huddled up at the edge of the lot most of the morning, drawing. I'd seen her, sketch pad in hand, the moment she got out of her car. Memories of the sketches that were always scattered around her house welled inside me. When inspiration struck, she'd sketch on a napkin, the back of a receipt, or anything else she could write on if her sketch pad wasn't in reach. Our first Christmas together, I'd given her a leather bound one.

Those memories burned in my chest. Thoughts of her grinning widely as she held up the sketch she'd made on a whim of the great room for our cabin were still fresh in my mind. The stone fireplace stretched two stories up in the vaulted space, and my mind had started spinning about what stone I'd use as soon as she showed it to me. She was the dreamer, and I was the one who made those dreams reality.

Or I had been, anyway. Now I was nothing to her. Just the contractor building the house she was doing the design work for. That was why I'd forced myself not to look her way all morning. I'd only snuck one glance, and she'd been focused on her drawing. I'd still taken in the view of the porcelain skin on her neck, which I could see since her hair was pulled up. How many times had I kissed that neck – and occasionally nipped at it – in the way that made her moan for more?

She'd been mine in every way, which was why losing her had crushed me. And as much as I wanted to hate her — or at the very least be apathetic — I couldn't. The overpowering urge to please and protect her was stronger than ever.

There was something new, too, and it scared me a little. I'd been attracted to Palmer from the moment I saw her. She'd made me wait months before we slept together, and I'd woken up with her on my mind every morning in anticipation. Even after we started having sex, she was the only woman I wanted anymore. But now when I looked at her, I felt a desire to ravage her that I'd never had before.

I wanted to own her body again, if only briefly. And I wasn't feeling very tender about it. My resentment over what happened between us had changed me, and I felt like a depraved asshole. I wanted to remind her – forcefully – that no man would ever know her body like I did.

When I pulled up to the job site, I stepped out of my truck and scanned the site for her. I needed to find a way to probe for information without seeming interested in her. The idea Derek had planted about her being sick had grown into a worry that wouldn't stop gnawing at me.

Hunter approached, finishing a bottle of water as he walked toward me.

"You lookin' for what's her name?"

"It's Palmer. Is she still here?"

He shook his head. "Left around noon."

I folded my arms across my chest, aggravated.

"Dammit," I muttered.

He knew better than to ask for details. And as much as I wanted to chase after Palmer, I couldn't let myself do it.

"I'm gonna inventory the framing materials," I said over my shoulder as I walked away. It was a perfect escape. There was no way I could work with the other guys in this pissed off, anxious mood. I needed to spend this afternoon alone with my thoughts.

Palmer

My heel slid deeper into the mud as I tried to dislodge my other shoe from the wet mess I'd gotten myself into.

So much for being inconspicuous. I'd hoped to slip into Derek and Adriane's house unnoticed so I could take photos and measurements in the area that would be their wine room. Instead I was heel-deep in a mud hole that was a lot squishier than it looked.

The guys on the crew were poking each other to point out my predicament and share a laugh over it. Jackasses.

I shifted my weight to one foot, trying to free the other shoe from the mud. I realized a second too late that I'd lost my balance. One of my shoes finally broke free from the mud as I tumbled over backwards.

I was waiting for the inevitable splash when a strong arm wrapped around my waist, pulling me up. Before I could even catch my breath, Brady was setting me on the gravel walkway.

"You alright?" he asked me.

I nodded, looking down at my mud-caked black shoes. "Thanks."

"You ladies need somethin' to do?" he yelled at the crew members who were still gawking at me. They scrambled, their grins disappearing in an instant.

"I'll take these off before I go inside," I promised, gesturing at my shoes.

"Don't do that, you might step on a nail," he said. "The dirt's not an issue, but you can wash them in the trailer if you want."

"I might, thanks. I'm going down to the wine room now."

Brady arched his brows, studying me. What was going on in his head right now? I was dying to know. Did he hate me? Still have some feelings? Or was he ambivalent?

"I better take you down," he said, taking off his baseball hat and running a hand through his hair. "No railings up on the staircase yet."

"Well, if anyone's likely to fall, it's me," I said, smiling. "You know how clumsy I am."

"It's those damn shoes," he said, shaking his head. "You can't wear heels at a construction site. And you're supposed to have a hard hat on."

"Where's yours?" I raised my brows in challenge.

"I know what's going on at all times on this site, so I don't need one."

"Hmm."

"Can you make it up to the house?" he asked with a glance at my feet.

"Sure."

I stepped gingerly across the rock pathway before walking through the open studs into the house. Brady was silent as he led the way to the basement stairs. I took advantage of the opportunity to stare at his shoulders and biceps, which were begging me to reach out and squeeze them. I'd left nail marks on his shoulders once that lasted a couple days.

My gaze wandered lower, to the perfect ass I'd also left nail marks in.

I stumbled on the last stair, too focused on his ass to remember what I was doing. Brady reached out and took my arm to support me.

"This is getting embarrassing," I said, my face heating.

He opened his mouth, looking like he was about to speak, but instead led the way across the basement to the future wine room.

I set my sketch pad on the floor and dug through my bag. Though I liked the nervous excitement of being near Brady again, I couldn't focus on work with him here.

"I thought ..." I murmured, rifling through old receipts, "I mean, I always keep a tape measure in here."

"You want mine?"

His dark gaze was locked on me, and my heart hammered with anticipation as he approached. When we were together, he'd looked at me with tender affection – never with this brooding intensity.

The tape measure was clipped to the pocket of his jeans, but he didn't reach for it when I nodded.

"Are you okay?"

His question was more like a demand. I swallowed hard, unable to hold his gaze.

"You mean from when I fell? I'm fine."

He took a step toward me, now so close I could smell the scent of fresh-cut wood on him. God, how I'd missed that. I breathed it in deeply, trying to be inconspicuous.

"No," he said, his voice softening a little. "What I mean is ... is something wrong? Are you sick? You've lost weight and you just don't look like yourself anymore."

My excitement twisted into a sinking sense of sadness. He still cared, which was nice, but his attraction to me was a thing of the past.

"No," I said, my hurt feelings evident in my tone. Dammit, I hated wearing my heart on my sleeve. "I'm not sick. My mom is, but you know that."

"Yeah. How is she?"

I shrugged. "Not good."

"I'm sorry, Palmer."

I looked up and our eyes met. My heart was now bouncing wildly in my chest, just from the nearness of him.

"It's why … I look like this," I said. "I'm taking care of Mom and Danny, and … I don't worry much about how I look."

He reached out a hand and rested it on my hip. I sucked in a breath, reeling from his touch. I wanted to be bold enough to reach for him in return, but I was frozen. I didn't want to move or speak for fear of breaking this spell and making him take his hand away.

"You're still beautiful," he said, his big hand closing around my hip. "Just thinner and maybe … more fragile."

I swallowed again, the compliment sending a wave of pleasure through my body, winding its way to every nerve ending.

Brady moved his other hand to my neck, cupping it from behind while his thumb stroked my jaw line. I let out a shaky breath, willing this moment to last.

Desire swirled in his emerald eyes, and he licked his lips.

"See, I might've been able to stop," he said in a low tone, "but I can see your nipples through your shirt, and now there's no way."

His words, and the feel of his hands on me, emboldened me to raise my chin in invitation. A smile played on his lips as he moved his thumb from my jaw line to my lips, running it over the top one, deliciously slowly, before moving on to the bottom one. I'd missed these rough-skinned hands on my skin so badly.

I reached around his waist, pressing myself forward, and he responded in an instant, his big arms pulling me into him as his mouth found mine. The solid warmth of him against me and the faint taste of coffee were achingly familiar and new all at once.

What started as a sweet reassurance quickly became something more. Brady's hands gripped my ass, lifting me and pressing me into his demanding, powerful erection. My body took over then, my tongue engaging in a power struggle with his while my hands pulled frantically at his hair.

Brady's teeth closed around my bottom lip, sending a surge downward to the ache between my thighs. I couldn't help grinding my hips into his, my body desperate for an end to the deep need he'd brought back to life in me.

I couldn't think past the feelings surging through me. The low groan I felt in Brady's chest told me I wasn't the only one who was incredibly turned on right now. Thank God we were alone down here, so we could ravage each other without anyone knowing.

"Brady?" a deep male voice called down the stairway.

I slid down Brady's body as we released each other. His guilty look of shock probably matched my own. We were supposed to be working.

"Uh …" Brady ran a hand through his hair and exhaled deeply. "What's up, Hunter?"

"Question on the plans," Hunter said.

"Be right up," Brady responded.

I ran my fingers over my lower lip, tender where Brady had bitten it. We just looked at each other for a few seconds before he closed his eyes briefly, turned and walked away.

Being interrupted was probably supposed to kill the mood, but I was still shaking with desire for him. I hadn't been kissed in nearly a year – since the last time he'd kissed me. But it wasn't just a kiss he'd left me wanting.

I smoothed out my clothes and hair, gathering myself. After a few minutes, I gathered my supplies and walked upstairs. There was no one in sight, so I tucked my sketch book under my arm and went straight for the door. I needed a long break from Brady before I'd be able to focus on work when he was anywhere nearby.

Chapter 7

Brady

Troy looked over as I put my truck in drive, and I took the opportunity to study his eyes for a second. They weren't red or glassy. I couldn't get a long enough look at his pupils, but I was pretty sure he wasn't high.

"What?" he asked defensively. "Stop lookin' at me like I'm your kid."

I shrugged. "You act like one sometimes."

"I've been clean since we moved to Colorado and you know it. We work so goddamn much it's not possible to have any fun."

"Yeah, but we came back home for this job. All the bad influences from before are close by again."

"Since when did you become such a tight ass?" he grumbled. "We used to drink together and have a good time."

"I grew up."

He gave me a knowing look. "It was when you got with Palmer. Never thought you'd lose your shit over such a good girl."

My skin tingled with awareness at the mention of her name. I'd jerked off last night and this morning thinking about that kiss. Probably would again tonight, too.

"I'm just not a dumbass," I said to Troy. "Obviously it wasn't just Palmer, because we aren't together anymore and I still keep my shit together. Unlike you."

He gave an agitated scoff and turned to me. "Speaking of Palmer, she's fuckin' hot. I was checking her out at work the other day."

"Shut the fuck up about her," I said, clenching the steering wheel.

"She was looking back, too. It's cool if I fuck her, right? You've been broken up long enough."

I shook my head, refusing to look at him. "I'm serious. Shut up, asshole."

"What is she, twenty-six? She's closer to my age than yours anyway. Next time she wears a dress, I'm gonna pull it up over her ass and fuck her 'til she screams my name."

I pulled the truck over and threw it into park. As soon as I had a free hand, I punched Troy in the shoulder.

"You don't know how to listen, do you, asshole? Don't even look at her."

His eyes, the same green as mine, brightened as he sneered at me. "What if she wants me? That'd be so rich. I'll bring her back to our place and make you listen through the walls."

I reached over and grabbed his shirt. He shoved a hand in my face to force me back.

"How does she like it?" he continued. "In the ass? Does she swallow?"

I was past anger now. Shoving him against the passenger door, I reached for the handle and pulled. He tumbled out, back first, with me on top of him.

We'd done this many times, but I'd never been this pissed off. I punched him in the nose, drawing blood. He reached up and rolled himself out from under me, panting as he took a swing and clipped me in the eye.

I was bigger, stronger and smarter. But Troy loved to fight. It was an outlet for his rage. We traded punches, oblivious to the world until a voice called out to us.

"Hey, what's going on over there?"

I glanced up and met the eyes of a graying woman who reminded me of my mom. She'd pulled over to the side of the road, arms crossed over her chest unhappily.

Troy used the opportunity to knee my groin.

"Asshole," I muttered.

The bystander was approaching now, and I got up from the ground.

"Everything's good," I said. "Thanks for stopping."

"You're bigger than him," she said, shaking a finger at me.

I tried not to smile as I replied. "That's true. In every way."

Troy pretended to scratch his face, covertly flipping me off.

"We'll be on our way," I said. "Thanks again."

We got back in the truck silently, both still exerted.

"I need a towel or something," Troy said. He had a hand pressed over his bleeding nose.

"Use your shirt, douchebag. You were asking for it."

"Bullshit. You're just pissed 'cause you know Palmer wants me to nail her."

I scowled at him, wanting to pull his ass back out of the truck, but the lady who'd scolded us was right behind me.

"She's not into loser drunks whose brothers have to babysit their every move," I said.

Troy's brow furrowed. "Christ, that hurts a little, man."

For once, he was serious. But I didn't feel sorry for him.

"Yeah, well it hurts that my own brother wants to fuck the only woman I've ever loved just to be an asshole."

"I'm not really gonna do it," he said in a sulky tone. "I'm just sayin', she's hot. Too bad you fucked that up."

His statement of the obvious made me shake my head with disgust. It *was* too bad. I'd wondered off and on if I'd overreacted during the conversation that led to me and Palmer breaking up. It had always nagged at me, but kissing her had brought the thought to the front of my mind again. I'd never wanted anyone the way I wanted her. She was worth waiting for. Not to mention that I'd bailed when she needed me most.

The what-ifs were haunting me now. What if I'd agreed to postpone the wedding and not been an asshole? What if I'd called her the next day and told her how sorry I was? What if I had put her needs before my pride?

I brooded the whole way to the prison, hoping Troy would give me a reason to lash out at him again. I hated that I'd lost Palmer, but it cut me to the bone to be honest with myself and admit it was my own fucking fault. I still remembered the look of shock on her face when I lost my shit and punched a hole in her wall. I'd turned a conversation about delaying the wedding into a breakup.

When I parked the truck, Troy and I got out and he followed me into the visitor's entrance. He was keeping his mouth shut now, which meant at least he was reading my mood well.

"Hi," I said to the guard behind the window. "Brady and Troy Grant. Here to see Tucker Grant."

The stocky guard looked from me to Troy, his face twisting with disbelief.

"You can't come in here like that," he said.

I had a fat lip and a swelling eye, but was otherwise fine. But when I looked at Troy, I saw that he wasn't. He had the bottom of his t-shirt pulled up to cover his nose, and it was smeared with blood, a dark spot of it growing larger by the second.

"You might wanna take him to a hospital," the guard suggested.

"He's fine," I said. "We'll go outside 'til the bleeding stops."

"He can't come in here with bloody clothes." The guard glared at me. "It's a bio-hazard."

"Okay." I nodded at Troy and we both headed for the door.

"I'm pretty broken up about not seeing the old man," Troy said in a deadpan as we walked to the truck.

I turned to him and we both busted out laughing. It felt good to let go of my built-up tension. When I clapped him on the shoulder, he cracked a smile.

"Alright," I said. "Let's go get a beer and shoot some pool. But no drugs or whores, got it?"

He shrugged. "No drugs I'm okay with. But you'll have to define whore for me, 'cause I'm horny as shit. I haven't gotten laid since we left home."

"You think of Colorado as home now?" I glanced at him and he shrugged.

"I guess. You mean more than Chicago feels like home?"

"Yeah."

"Home's wherever I lay my head down at night," he said. "You like being back here?"

"Yeah, I do. It's good to see Mom again, and … Derek. I've gotten to hang out with him a couple times."

Troy gave me a skeptical glare. "You weren't gonna say Derek, you were gonna say Palmer."

"Fuck off."

"You better not be a dick at the bar. I won't get any ass if you're a lousy wingman."

I shook my head. "I thought we were going so we can have a beer together."

"You come off like a brooding asshole. Don't do that."

I spotted a bar and slowed the truck down. "You wanna just go alone?"

"No." He turned away from me, staring out the window of the truck. "Are we gonna go back and see Dad sometime?"

"If you want to."

He shrugged silently. I pulled into a parking place and put the truck in park.

"I go back and forth on Dad," I admitted. "Sometimes I hate the bastard. There's plenty of reasons to. But then other times ... I kinda miss him. I had a question about codes here the other day that I know he'd have the answer for. Had to look that shit up in my code book."

"Yeah, me too," Troy said, still staring out the window. "If I feel anything nice for him, I get pissed at myself. He fucked over the people who trusted him."

"It'd go a long way with me if he was at least sorry. His selfishness is sort of epic. He spent so much time riding our asses about being good men, and it turns out he's not one himself."

Troy grunted his agreement and I reached for his shoulder and squeezed it. "Nose done bleedin'?"

He nodded and looked over at me.

"I believe you when you say you're still clean," I said. "And I'm damn proud of you."

The corners of his mouth turned up in a smile. "Buy me a beer then, asshole."

"You got it. I'll even kick your ass at pool if you want."

I missed his sarcastic reply as I climbed out of my truck and shut the door. Would we go back to the prison to visit Dad? I wasn't sure. But I sure as hell wasn't sorry our trip to see him had been cut short. Let him be the one disappointed for a change.

Palmer

I parked my car on the side of the gravel road at Derek and Adriane's house, pulled a travel size perfume from my bag and rolled it on to my wrist. The sweet fragrance made me instantly feel prettier. I checked my hair in the mirror and stepped out of the car, careful to steady my heels on the rocks to avoid a fall.

It was crazy to have butterflies in my stomach over Brady. We'd been through so much, so why did it feel like I had a crush on him all of a sudden? I'd been looking forward to seeing him all morning at work. The feel of his warm lips on mine was still fresh. I reached up and touched them softly as I remembered the way his tongue had brushed over mine.

The anticipation was killing me. I took a deep breath and turned toward the house. I'd only made it a couple steps when the engine of Brady's huge black pickup truck started. He was driving down the makeshift road to leave the site, and my butterflies made a crash landing of disappointment.

He slowed as he approached and I made eye contact, about to wave when he stopped his truck.

"Hey," he said, resting his elbow on the door since the window was down.

"Hi." I stood next to the truck, admiring the bronzed, muscled arm on display in front of me.

"How are you?"

"Good. Are you leaving?"

"Yeah." He took off his baseball hat and ran a hand through his dark, sweaty hair. "Have to go shop for materials."

I willed him to ask me to join him. The passenger seat of his truck had a stack of papers and a t-shirt on it. I wanted to be right there, next to Brady. Riding next to him in the truck had always reinforced his masculinity to me. Plus, it smelled like him.

On the verge of making a comment about how much I liked shopping, I closed my mouth when he gave me a lopsided grin.

"This is random, but did you ever get that hole in your kitchen wall fixed?" he asked.

I shook my head, my heart sinking at his mention of *the fight*. I only spent one night a week at my house these days – Friday night, when my aunt and uncle made the hour trip to stay with Mom and Danny so I could have a break. I'd refused their offer initially, but fortunately, they'd refused my refusal. It was good to have a night that belonged only to me.

"Um, no," I said. "But it's not a big deal, really. I'm hardly there."

"Oh." His face hardened and I realized he probably thought I spent my nights with another man.

"Because I stay at my mom's house six nights a week," I blurted. "To take care of her and Danny. That's why I'm hardly at home."

His eyes softened. "Can I fix the wall?"

I waved him off and shook my head. "It's not a big deal, Brady. Really."

"I want to. It's a simple drywall patch. Just let me know when's a good time."

My mind was reeling. Brady was coming to my house. The house we'd planned to share. The house we'd gone to bed and woken up together in so many times. The house we'd broken up in.

"Well, Friday nights are the only time I'm there." I tucked my hair behind my ear, needing to occupy my hands.

"You open this Friday night?"

I nodded.

"Is seven o'clock okay?" He put the hat back on and I just nodded again. I'd never been the polished, put-together woman who knew how to flirt with men. Especially not this one, who made me forget anyone else even existed.

"See you then," he said with a nod.

"Sure." I waved and turned back toward the house. His truck tires crunched over the gravel and my insides clenched with arousal. A year without sex had made me into a woman who responded sexually to Brady's *truck*. Or maybe it was the memory of a heated make out session we'd had in his vehicle after a date once. Either way, Brady and his truck would be at my house tomorrow night, and I could hardly wait.

Brady

I raised my hand to knock on Palmer's door, pausing. I'd never knocked on this door. We were already together when she bought the house, and I'd just walked in from the time she moved in.

But the ex fiancé definitely shouldn't walk in, so I knocked. My subconscious was screaming in my head as I waited, reminding me that this was a shitty idea of epic proportions. I hadn't been able to keep my hands off Palmer while at work – what would I do when we were alone in her house?

Even though she'd melted into me when I kissed her, I was still pissed at myself. We were over. It had taken me a long-ass time to move on from our breakup, and I couldn't go back to being hung up on her.

She opened the door and gave me the shy smile I remembered from when we were first dating. Cutoff jean shorts on Palmer had always been my undoing. She wore them with a gray t-shirt that hugged her slender curves, her feet bare and her long brown hair loose around her shoulders.

I clenched the handle on the bucket of supplies I carried.

I'm here to patch the fucking drywall. Just patch the drywall and then get the hell out of here.

"Hey, come in," she said.

Conflicting emotions pulled at me as I walked through the small living room and into the kitchen.

We'd made out on that green couch so many times, starting with heated kissing and graduating to my hands exploring every inch of her body. I knew exactly what she liked before we ever slept together.

She'd picked up the carved walnut floor lamp at a flea market we went to one weekend. Her whole face lit up when she saw it. I'd hauled that fucker more than a mile back to my truck. When we stopped for dinner on the way home that night, I kept one eye on the truck the whole time, worried someone would take the lamp she'd fallen in love with.

The oak table in the kitchen sucked the warmth from my chest. She'd been sitting there when she ripped my heart from my chest, saying she didn't need me. It wasn't her saying she wanted to move back the wedding that still haunted me, it was that one sentence: *"I want you here, but I don't need you here."*

Nothing had ever made me feel weaker than needing someone who didn't need me back.

"So, how was your day?" Palmer asked, opening the fridge and holding up a bottle of my favorite dark beer in question.

I nodded and reached for it. This was way too much like old times for my comfort.

"Good. I'll be out of your hair soon. I'll have to come back and sand the mud after it dries. Maybe next Friday night."

"Sure. Thanks for doing this." She opened a drawer and withdrew a bottle opener, using it on the bottle of beer in her hand.

I forced myself not to smile, because one – she hated beer. And two – the caps twisted off, but she didn't know that. Novice.

"Anything I can do to help?" she asked, sipping the beer. When she cringed, I had to smile.

"Wanna make me a steak?" I said, teasing.

Her brows shot up hopefully. "I have the stuff to grill some burgers if you're hungry."

When she reached up to gather her hair in her hands, her shirt hiked up a little and I caught a glimpse of her smooth, flat stomach. My cock stiffened in response and I forced my eyes away.

"You don't have to make me dinner, Palmer."

"Well, I haven't eaten, and if you haven't, we might as well eat, right?"

I shrugged, sorting through my dry wall tools. "If you feel like it, sure."

She broke out in a grin and grabbed the beer bottle, sipping again and cringing again.

"You develop a taste for dark beer?" I asked as I measured the hole my fist had made.

"Not really. I just … bought it and thought I'd give it a go."

I was pretty sure she'd bought it for me, which brought on more warring emotions. It was a nice gesture, but this woman had power over me, and it was dangerous to forget it.

She busied herself getting the food ready and I tried to focus my attention on the wall repair. My eyes wandered over to her ass and legs, easy for me to admire openly since her back was to me as she worked at the counter.

"You got anything else needing fixed?" I asked. "This won't take long."

She glanced at me over her shoulder. "The closet door in my bedroom is broken. The handle, actually. It won't latch anymore."

"I'll look at it." She turned around and I snuck another glance at her ass. "What about your mom's? She need anything done?"

Palmer's shoulders sank. "Things have really fallen by the wayside over there."

"Shouldn't be anything I can't handle," I said, taking a long pull of my beer. "What needs to be done?"

She was silent for a few seconds. I set my drywall saw down and turned my attention her way. "Palmer?"

"I'm sorry," she said, her voice strained with emotion. "It's just … I'm not sure what I'm even going to do with her house. Her treatment options are exhausted. Now it's only a matter of time. There's no reason for you to come do a bunch of work on her house if I won't even be keeping it."

I was powerless. Nothing could keep me from walking across the kitchen to her. She turned around and let me wrap her up in my arms.

"I'm sorry," I said in her ear. "I'm so sorry, Palmer. I wish you'd told me."

"I don't want you to feel sorry for me," she said, her voice muffled against my chest.

"It's not that I feel sorry for you. I know there's nothing I can do, but I always loved your mom and Danny."

"They always loved you, too." She pulled back and looked up at me, and I could see she was struggling with something.

"What is it?" I asked.

"It's …" She sighed softly, considering. "When I wake up in the morning, I jump out of bed and run to check on my mom. I worry that she'll go in her sleep suddenly. And that worry is with me every waking second. I worry that the home health aide will call and tell me she died and I wasn't there. Or that something awful will happen to her in front of Danny and he'll be traumatized. I worry at work, I worry when I'm racing through the aisles of the grocery store and when I'm taking a shower."

I ran my fingers over the long, soft hair I'd missed so much. She met my eyes and continued.

"The only time I've been awake and not worried – the only time in weeks that's happened – was when you kissed me the other day."

I bent to rest my forehead against hers, cupping a hand around the back of her neck. I felt her sharp intake of breath and knew I was in way over my head.

"When I kissed you the other day, you were so responsive. Starved for it. When's the last time you were kissed properly?"

Her skin heated in response to the question. "It's been a while. Sorry."

I cupped her soft cheeks in my palms. "Don't apologize. You set me on fire, Palmer. Always have."

"You do the same to me," she said in a breathy whisper.

"Listen … With your mom, you'll have some warning," I said softly. "I remember how it was with my uncle. The doctors will make sure she slides out of life peacefully at the end. Don't do this to yourself."

"I don't know what else to do," she said, choking on the words. "Working and worrying and planning … those things keep me sane."

I brushed the hair back from her ear and let my lips wander behind it for a kiss – a soft, lingering kiss that made her breath catch.

"God, Brady," she said, putting her hand over mine, which was resting on her hip. She guided it beneath her shirt, to the soft, perfect stomach I'd been admiring earlier.

I wound my fingers around a section of her hair, tipping her face up to me. Her hazel eyes were begging for more. My logic didn't stand a chance. I wanted her, and I wanted to make her feel good even more.

When my lips met hers, she reached around my back and gripped it hard, pressing her body to mine. I took her hands and guided them above her head, allowing me to pull her t-shirt off in a quick motion.

She lunged at me, her expression desperate and hungry. I caught her in my arms and she wrapped her legs around my waist. I kissed her hard, biting her lip the way she'd responded to the other day. When she fisted my hair and jerked my head back, diving close to kiss and nip my neck, I shoved her against the kitchen counter and forced her legs further apart.

At her moan of encouragement, I grabbed her ass and pulled her body against my raging erection. That brought forth a louder moan, and I pulled her hair back again, the bounce of her small tits in her lacy white bra making my cock so hard it pulsed.

"You wanna get fucked?" I asked in a low tone. Her glazed eyes found mine and she nodded, her lips parted with desire.

I smiled, my position of control giving me a heady, hot sensation.

"I've never fucked you, Palmer. I made love to you many times, but we never fucked. You sure you want it?"

"Yes." Her pleading tone reminded me that for once, I had the upper hand.

"I'm gonna fuck you right here on your kitchen counter. It'll be a rough ride. I'm not gonna kiss you or whisper in your ear. But you'll come hard, I promise you that."

"Yes," she cried. "Please, Brady. Fuck me."

I groaned and rubbed my cock, which was about to bust out of my jeans. "Baby, that sounds so hot coming from your sweet mouth."

She pulled my t-shirt off and reached for the button on my jeans, her chest flushed with desire. I'd never seen this side of Palmer, and damned if it wasn't the hottest thing ever. I unbuttoned and slid off her jean shorts, taking off her little white panties next.

While I pulled a condom from my wallet and stepped out of my jeans, she unhooked her bra and tossed it to the floor. The sight of her, sitting naked on the kitchen counter, her legs spread in anticipation of my cock, was unbelievably hot.

She wasn't feeling worried now. Her face said it all – she felt sexy and way too hot to feel anything but this moment we were in. I'd done that – taken away her hurt and anxiety, and that was the headiest feeling of all.

Her cry when I slammed my cock into her was a frenzied sound of alarm and pain. Damn, her pussy was tight, squeezing my cock like a vise. I had to take a second to get my bearings.

"Christ, baby," I said under my breath, "Been a while?"

"About a year," she said, her voice shaking. My eyes went right to hers as my shock registered.

"Are you fuckin' serious? Not since me?"

She shook her head, her cheeks warming with what looked like shame.

I covered her mouth with mine, kissing her deep. My chest felt like it was about to burst.

"You're the only man I've ever wanted," she said, on the verge of tears.

"*Fuck*, Palmer." I thrust myself into her hard, promising myself to give it to her good before I got close to getting off. She clung to me, her legs wrapped tight around my waist. It only took about a half dozen deep thrusts before I felt her pussy start to spasm around my cock.

"Oh, God, Brady," she cried, her nails digging into my shoulders. Tears fell from the corners of her eyes as she came so violently I felt every second of it. I was right behind her, groaning loudly as I buried myself in her one last time. An intense shockwave hit my whole body, making me drop my head into Palmer's neck, slack with satisfaction.

The common sense my cock had overpowered returned with full force. It wasn't getting off that had me feeling so satisfied – it was Palmer. I hadn't just given in to my attraction to her, I'd bowed to her need for comfort. And when she'd told me I was the only man she'd ever wanted, I'd felt that deep, desperate pull to her again.

The pull that had taken me months to get over. I was a sucker for punishment.

"Dammit," I said, grabbing my jeans from the floor.

"What?" Palmer slid down from the counter, wrapping her arms around her naked body.

"I can't do this, Palmer," I said. "I moved on."

She picked up her t-shirt and slid into it.

"I don't understand. I thought we both wanted that."

"Yeah, but … there are much easier fucks out there for both of us," I said, zipping my jeans and scrubbing a hand down my face.

Her lips parted with shock. "Easier fucks? Is that what you've been doing since we broke up? Just fucking random women?"

I shrugged. "Yeah, so what? We broke up a year ago. You expected me to just never fuck anyone else?"

Her expression closed off and she reached for her shorts, stepping into them.

"Well, I haven't," she said.

"You've had your mind elsewhere," I said, aggravated.

"How many?" she asked, her eyes locked on mine.

I pulled my t-shirt over my head and glared at her. "How many?"

"Yeah. How many women have you fucked?"

I couldn't believe she had the nerve to ask me that. "You mean counting you, just now?"

She pulled back her hand to slap me and I caught her wrist with little effort, lowering it gently.

"It doesn't matter," I said.

"Just own it." Her voice wavered. "Tell me."

It was my chance to hurt her, and I got a sick satisfaction from being honest about it. "I don't know, maybe a dozen?"

She drew back, visibly shocked. "So while I've been caring for my dying mother, you've been fucking *a dozen* other women?"

"You didn't want me! What the fuck is this? You're acting like I cheated on you or something."

"No." She swiped her palms across her cheeks. "You didn't owe me anything. But it's ironic that you accused me of cheating that day when you're the only man I've ever been with. Then you—"

"We weren't together!" I roared, my patience fading by the second.

"I didn't stop caring about you," she said. "Apparently you forgot me the moment you walked out the door. And it hurts, Brady. Thinking about you with all those other women ... it fucking *hurts*."

"Does that mean we're even? Because you fuckin' broke me, Palmer, when you said you didn't need me."

"I think it means you're still an asshole."

I shook my head, picking up the used condom and tossing it in the trash. I threw my tools in the bucket I brought.

"I'll finish another time," I muttered.

"The night's young. Still plenty of time to go find a random at a bar," she said, her tone cold.

I wanted to swallow her back up in my arms and tell her she had it all wrong. The other women weren't about forgetting her – they were about being unable to.

But I couldn't. Damned if I'd expose myself to her that way when she was being so fucking mean. I just headed for the front door and walked out, closing it behind me without looking back.

Chapter 8

Palmer

Danny's big yawn as I helped him get his sweatpants pulled up brought on a yawn from me, too.

"We can't be doing that," I said, grinning. "It's only seven-thirty in the morning."

I helped him sit down on the edge of the bed and he looked around the room, eyes wide. "Where's Mom?"

"She's sleeping. Let's be quiet so we don't wake her up, okay?"

Last night Mom had spaced out several times during dinner, and she hadn't eaten a bite. I could tell Danny was worried about her, whether he said anything about it or not. And I had no idea what to say. Reassuring him felt wrong, because she was not okay. But I didn't think he understood the concept of death, and I didn't know how to explain it to him.

"You want oatmeal?" I asked, pushing his wheelchair up to the edge of the bed. He nodded and yawned again.

"Did you stay up late last night watching baseball?" I bent to help him into his chair, trying to lift with my legs. But he was almost twice my size, and damn, was he heavy.

"Cubs," he said.

"Well, of course." I smiled when he batted my hand away so he could wheel his chair into the kitchen instead of letting me do it. "And who won?"

"Cubs," he echoed, grinning. In his world, the Cubs won every game. I loved that. In fact, I'd started DVRing games so I could replay them on nights there wasn't a game on. Soon the Cubs would win every night of the week in our home.

"Amanda will be here soon," I said, grabbing oatmeal and fruit to make breakfast.

"Manda," Danny said.

"She's nice, right?" I looked at him, trying to gauge his reaction. He smiled, which meant yes.

The home health aide I'd hired was a godsend. She worked second shift as a CNA at a home for the disabled nearby. Since she struggled to make ends meet, she was also working days taking care of Mom and Danny. She was capable and very sweet, spending lots of one on one time with my brother.

I stared into the pan of water on the stove as tiny bubbles started to form, waiting for it to boil.

"Danny, what am I gonna do about Brady?" I said, watching the bubbles rise to the surface.

"Brady!" he cried.

"Yes. He gave me a pretty ring, remember? I've missed him a lot. And seeing him again makes me think about him all the time. But I shut him out when he wanted to be there for me, and I don't think he can forgive me."

"Almer," Danny said, opening his arms. He'd been pronouncing my name that way since we were kids. I walked over and hugged him tight.

"That was just what I needed, little brother."

The doorbell rang and when I opened it, Amanda greeted me with a smile.

"Morning," she said, stepping in. She was a tall, curvy girl with a blonde pixie cut that was always damp from her morning shower when she arrived.

"Morning," I said. "I made coffee."

"I love you."

She headed straight for the kitchen.

"Hey, Danny," she said. "I brought a game for us to play. And I brought pudding, too."

"Pudding!"

"Damn right. Chocolate fudge, butterscotch or vanilla. Whoever wins *The Price is Right* gets to choose."

I smiled. They played along with the game show every day. Amanda was such a breath of fresh air for all of us.

"Mom's still in bed," I said, pouring coffee into my travel mug. "She had some ... unclear moments last night."

"I'll go check on her," Amanda said. "When's her next doctor appointment?"

"Wednesday."

She nodded. "Have a good day. We've got it all under control here, don't we, Danny?"

"Cubs," he proclaimed.

"You've got that right," I heard Amanda saying to him as I waved and headed for the door. "But we need to talk about their pitching last night."

I dialed Georges on my way to the office, setting my phone on the seat and putting in on speakerphone.

"Hey, stranger," he said. "What's up with us not talking all weekend?"

"Just busy. How was your weekend?"

"So good. I went to the flea market and an auction Saturday and scored some awesome pieces for Adriane's house. Met a cute guy at the coffee shop Saturday night, met him for lunch Sunday."

"That's great," I said. "Details?"

"Not much to tell. His name's Logan and he's a trust fund baby in grad school. We're going out Friday night. How was your weekend?"

I paused a second and dove in. "Good. You know, took care of Mom and Danny, did my laundry and had sex with Brady."

"WHAT?" His squeal made me roll my eyes as I eased to a stop at a red light.

"Yeah, it happened and it did not end well," I said, sighing.

"You didn't come?" Georges sounded scandalized, and I couldn't help laughing.

"Oh no, I came alright. That part was epic. But we got into a fight after, and I was kind of a bitch."

"Why would you be a bitch after epic sex?"

"Because he regretted it, and that hurt my feelings."

Georges grunted his agreement. "Well, tell me the good stuff. How'd it go down?"

"Uh, on my kitchen counter."

"You bad girl," he said, amused.

"Yeah. He told me we were going to fuck, and that we'd never fucked before, we'd only made love."

"I just broke out in a sweat," Georges said.

"Yeah. And we did, and it was amazing."

"It's about fucking time. I've told you this whole time that you seem to be waiting for him."

I sighed and rubbed my forehead. "No, Georges. I've been taking care of my family. And he has most definitely not been waiting for me."

"What do you mean?"

"He said he's screwed a dozen women since we broke up."

"Well, you guys are broken up, and he is a hot, single straight man. Can't say I blame him."

"I don't want to talk about it anymore."

"If he knew how you feel—"

I cut in. "Georges, *I* don't even know how I feel. Are we meeting with the Stanhopes this morning?"

"Yes, at nine."

"And the presentation is ready?"

"It's gonna rock their socks off."

"Great. I'll be there soon, okay? Want me to stop and get you a cappuccino?"

"Do I even have to answer that?"

I smiled. "On it. See you in a few."

I focused my mind on the Stanhopes' great room renovation. Fortunately, I didn't need to go to Derek and Adriane's house today. I had a nagging desire to go anyway, because I wasn't proud of some of the comments I'd made to Brady. But it would have to wait. Today I needed to catch up on work for my other clients.

Brady

I fed a sheet of English oak into the planer, the familiar hum of the machine at work easing away a little of my tension. If the weekend had felt long, today had been a lot longer.

It wasn't Palmer I was pissed at as much as myself, but I'd sure as hell taken it out on her. She hadn't been coming on to me, she'd been crying about her mom. I was the one who approached her and made it into something more.

I'd gone back and forth in my head all weekend about whether she'd come to the site today. I could've just called her to talk about things, but instead I'd brooded until I boiled over today, bitching at the guys over mundane shit that normally didn't bother me.

And now I was at my dad's old workshop, creating a bench at 10 pm when I should've been at home. Troy and I were staying at a small studio apartment while we did this job. But tonight I'd felt like coming to the place that felt more like home – the place I'd grown up in.

My dad had taught me woodworking in this shop, starting with scrap wood and working up to beautiful, exotic woods we made furniture from. We'd rarely talked when we were in the workshop – we just both did our thing. Yet those were the times I'd felt closest to him. Dad was a natural teacher; he always pointed out how I could improve on my skills. When he stopped commenting, I felt pride at having mastered the art he'd taught me.

There was no room in my thoughts for resentment of him right now. I was only thinking of Palmer. She was avoiding me. And as much as I hated it, that was best for both of us. I had to keep my shit together. As soon as Derek's house was done, I was going back to Colorado. Business was great there, Troy was able to stay clean and life was a whole lot easier.

The door to the workshop opened with a creak and my mom stuck her head in.

"Brought you some dinner," she said. I nodded and she walked in with a plate of meatloaf and mashed potatoes.

"You don't have to stay up just because I'm here," I said. "I'll be staying late."

"It's already late. And I like staying up late because you're here."

She set the plate on a workbench and I walked over to eat.

"Thanks. I'm starving."

"What's going on with you?" Mom pulled up a chair and sat down. I didn't remember her dark brown hair having the streaks of gray I saw in it now. Probably Dad's fault.

I shrugged, occupying myself with the food.

"Brady, I know you too well to believe you just had a hankering for woodworking at this hour. This is your outlet. It was always your dad's, too."

"Here's hoping we don't have any more than that in common," I muttered.

"Is that what's bothering you? Are people giving you problems now that you're back home for this job?"

I shook my head, sinking into a chair across from her. "It's Palmer. She's the interior designer for Derek's house."

"Oh."

Silence hung in the air for several seconds.

"This is really good," I said after swallowing a bite of meatloaf.

"Talk to me, Brady. You keep everything inside and it's not good. Tell me how you're feeling about seeing Palmer again."

I ran a hand through my hair, considering. Mom and I had always had an open relationship, but there were some things no one wanted to discuss with their mother.

"It's rough."

"Are there still feelings there?"

I considered as I chewed. "Yeah. It's actually worse than feelings still being there. They're stronger than they were before."

"Why is that bad?"

"Because I don't like her having any kind of control over me. She broke my heart, remember?"

Mom's lips curved up slightly. "Didn't you break hers, too?"

"She didn't leave me much choice."

"I find that hard to believe. She was so in love with you. And you always tended to get emotional when it came to her. Did you overreact, maybe?"

I wrinkled my brow in a glare. "Whose side are you on here? You know what happened. She told me her mom was sick and there wasn't room for me anymore. What could I have done?"

"You could've let the news sink in. That was the day her mother got diagnosed with a terminal illness, Brady. Who's thinking rationally on a day like that? You could've comforted her and reassured her."

I sighed deeply and met Mom's gaze. "*Should've*, you mean? I should've done that?"

She arched her brows in question. "What do you think?"

"Yeah. I flew off the handle and I shouldn't have. But I thought she'd call and we'd be able to talk it through some more."

"She probably thought you'd call. So a great love ended over stubbornness?"

"It sure as hell never ended for me," I said, running a hand through my hair. "But I resent her now."

"Resentment gets you nowhere."

I shrugged. "It is what it is. I resent her."

"Does she resent you?"

"I don't know."

"And which means more to you – loving her or resenting her?"

I folded my arms across my chest, unable to come up with an answer.

"I had to ask myself that question after your father started his prison term," she said. "I was numb during the arrest and trial part. But after he left, I had nothing but time on my hands. Didn't want to leave the house because I was too ashamed to show my face. And I thought about things a lot."

"And what'd you come up with?"

"I decided that even though he is a very flawed man, he is *my* flawed man. My husband. We have work ahead of us, but our marriage is worth it."

I tried to keep the bitterness from my voice when I spoke, but it was impossible. "And it doesn't bother you that he isn't sorry? He stole money that wasn't his, screwed people out of their retirement funds and left me with a huge mess. And all he thought about was *himself*. His appeal."

"Have you seen him since you got back?"

I shook my head with disgust.

"You should go see him," she said, reaching for my empty plate. "Not for him. For you."

I watched her back, covered with a fluffy purple bath robe, as she headed for the garage door.

"Did you make that meatloaf just for me?"

She turned and smiled. "Of course I did. I miss having someone to cook for."

"You can cook for me anytime."

"Will you bring Palmer by for dinner sometime?"

The thought made me shift uncomfortably. Hooking up was one thing, but bringing her back to see my mom again? That was another.

"We'll see," I said, turning back to my project.

Palmer

The rain pounding on Mom's roof was long overdue. I relished the sound of it, knowing it meant I wouldn't have to hand water the flowers I'd planted in pots next to her driveway.

I'd cleaned up from dinner and Danny was immersed in a baseball game on TV. When I headed for the front door, I felt a sense of gratitude for this moment. Mom was feeling good tonight, and she was sitting on the front porch swing, watching the rain.

She looked at me and smiled when I walked out and sat down next to her. Cancer was waging a battle against her body, but her eyes were the same hazel swirl of warmth I'd always known.

"Hey," I said.

"Hi there. How are you holding up?"

"Me? I'm good."

We swung in silence for a few seconds, a light mist from the downpour hitting my face even though the porch had an awning.

"There's something about dying that makes me think about my life," Mom said softly.

My chest tightened. I wanted to press my hands over my ears or get up and walk away. No matter what the doctors said, I couldn't let my mind consider what she was saying. She was sick, but she was still here. That was what I focused on every day.

She turned her lean face toward me. "I shortchanged you. Even though I love you and Danny the same, I always gave him more of my time."

I scoffed and looked away. "Mom, don't say that. You had to give him more time. He needed you more."

"I told myself that at the time, too. But ..." She shook her head sadly. "Do you remember that dance recital when you were in fourth grade?"

Of course I remembered, but why did she want to talk about it now? It was so long ago, and it was *over*.

"All the mothers got together to make the girls purple tutus with sequins. They used tulle – miles of it – so the skirts poufed out. But I couldn't leave Danny for the evening, so I picked up a tutu at the store for you."

She didn't need to describe the tutu – I could still see it in my mind. It had actually just been a purple skirt. I'd been mortified when my dance teacher looked at it, brows arched with disdain, and asked where my tutu was. I'd mumbled an excuse about forgetting it, my cheeks flaming with embarrassment.

"I didn't even go to the recital," Mom said, sighing deeply and staring at the oak tree in her tiny back yard. "I think Danny was having a meltdown that night and I was afraid to go, so I just dropped you off."

I cut in defensively. "It wasn't that you *didn't* go, Mom, it was that you couldn't. If anyone's to blame, it's Dad, for ditching his family when the going got tough. You did your best."

She reached for my hand and squeezed it. "I'm sure it didn't feel that way to the little girl who was alone at her recital wearing the wrong skirt."

I pressed my lips together, forcing back the emotion that rose in my throat. "Let's not dwell on anything like that," I said. "How about some iced tea?"

Though she nodded, her face fell with a hint of disappointment. "Sure, that sounds nice."

I went into the house to brew fresh tea, cracking ice cubes out of their trays while I waited, then wiping down the kitchen counters again for good measure.

When I stopped next to the island and rested my hands on it, emotion flooded me. God, this was *hard*. I wasn't equipped for any of it. My mom was my rock during hard times, and I wanted to fill that role for her now, but damned if I knew how.

Closing my eyes, I took a few calming breaths. It wasn't time to cry yet. I could hold out for a couple more hours. In the sanctuary of the basement, I'd cry until I was a hiccupping mess.

I pulled glasses from the cabinet and set to finding the teabags. Right now, I was going to be good company to Mom on this rainy summer evening.

Chapter 9

Palmer

The butterflies were back. When I spotted Brady's truck parked on the side of the gravel road at Derek and Adriane's house, there was no stopping the fluttering in my stomach. It had been six days since I'd seen him, but it felt like forever.

When I approached the house, Brady was talking to one of his employees, gesturing how to do something with his hands. He gave me a sidelong glance as I walked past him and went in the house.

What was he thinking? Was he struggling with mixed emotions, too? I'd been bothered by thoughts of him with other women all weekend. And I'd wondered how I stacked up to the ones he'd been with since me. Probably not that great, since he was my first and only.

I was on my way to the wine room when I heard footsteps behind me on the stairway. I waited at the bottom, and Brady came hustling down at a pace that definitely would've made me fall, his heavy boots pounding against the wood stairs.

"Can you make an effort to dress more professionally when you're on site?" he said in a growl.

I wrinkled my face in confusion, glancing down at my gray pencil skirt, black open-toed heels and purple cap-sleeved shirt.

"Professional?" I looked back up and met his gaze. "What's unprofessional about this?"

"You're showing too much skin." He arched his brows in judgment.

"What?" I glared at him. "Just my arms, Brady."

"And your legs."

I rolled my eyes. "Women have been wearing skirts in the workplace for decades, you caveman."

"Not at construction sites, sweetheart. It's distracting to my crew."

"I seriously doubt my skirt is distracting anyone."

Brady leaned closer and I felt the heat of his body near mine. "It's distracting me."

I scoffed as though I doubted it, but my heart was pounding like mad. Was he saying he still liked what he saw? I'd stopped feeling like a woman a long time ago. My life consisted of working, caring for my family and sleeping. No one looked at me the way Brady was looking right now – eyes dark, gaze hungry. Maybe I'd been more than just the closest woman in reach the other night.

"What do you want me to wear?" I asked weakly, trying to think of something – anything — besides throwing myself against him like an animal in heat.

"Jeans and sleeves would be a great start. And tennis shoes."

I cocked my brows at him. "This isn't the only job I'm doing. I have meetings with clients. I can't wear jeans and tennis shoes."

He shook his head, obviously frustrated. "I've never had to deal with being hard at work, Palmer. Can you help me out and dress more conservatively? And stop wearing that perfume?"

"Oh." I bit my lip, trying not to smile. Looking at me had made him hard. It was impossible not to smile.

"It's not fucking funny, you vixen," he muttered, running a hand through his hair.

I laughed and gave him an apologetic glance. "I'm sorry. It's not like you think. It's just ... I'm the furthest thing from a vixen. And I'm kind of floored that even though I haven't been to a hair salon in several months and I'm wearing clothes I've owned for *years*, you still think I'm worth looking at."

"I did a lot more than look the other night."

My face flushed as I remembered it. The way he'd pulled my hair and pounded himself into me with no mercy had made me feel sexier than I ever had. Knowing I brought that out of him brought the same primal desires from me, too.

"You loved it, didn't you?" he said, a cocky grin lighting up his whole face. "Say it."

"I did," I said, unable to meet his gaze. "Couldn't you tell?"

He stepped closer, speaking in a low tone. "No, *say it*, baby. Say you loved me fucking you."

I raised my chin and locked eyes with him, willing myself to be bold. "I loved you fucking me. I didn't know it could hurt and feel so good at the same time."

He ran a hand through his hair and sighed deeply. "I ride my brother's ass all the time about drugs, but you know what? *You're my drug.* You've been on my mind nonstop since Friday night. I crave you, Palmer. No one else. My heart's always belonged to you, and you broke it, but there's something about knowing your body belongs to me that makes it feel just a little bit better."

My head swam and my heart hammered uncontrollably. Even after being apart so long, he still felt something. I didn't care if it was only physical – at least that was something.

"Please kiss me," I said, my voice nearly a whisper. He put his large hand on my chin and jaw line, tipping my face up to meet his, and kissed me soft and slow. It was the opposite of the other night. No biting. No pain. Just his tongue dancing lazily with mine, making me want more.

I reached for the bulge in his pants and stroked his stiff erection.

"I'm sorry for some of the things I said the other night," I said. "I've got no right to be bitter about you being with other women."

A smile tugged up the corner of his lips. "You think I could want any other woman after fucking you like that, Palmer? I've jerked off every night since just thinking about it. No other women. Not if I can have you."

I exhaled with relief and unbuttoned his jeans. "Let me make it up to you."

With a small groan, Brady guided my hand away from his erection. "No."

"Oh." My face warmed with embarrassment. "I'm sorry."

"Don't misread me," he said, reaching for a lock of my hair and running his fingers over it. "I would love to see you in front of me on your knees, but not here. Not at work."

I bit my lip, feeling chastised.

"Lunch?" he asked, running a thumb over my lip. "In my truck?"

I nodded, my skin heating at the thought of being close to him again. I craved him, too. Whether it was right or wrong, a good idea or a bad one, I wanted the escape from sadness that only his body could provide.

"Meet me at noon," he said, turning back to the stairway. I glanced at my watch as he walked back upstairs. Only two hours of forcing myself to think about designing this basement.

Brady

Her hair was pulled back in a bun as she approached the truck wearing an expression that was an attempt at coolness. I knew better, though. Those dark brown eyes and the flushed skin on her neck gave her away.

"Hungry?" I asked, opening the passenger side door for her. Her cheeks pinked as she nodded and stepped in.

Everyone on this job site could see us leaving together. My guys were probably making lewd comments from the tables they sat at near the trailer for lunch break. I didn't care. Sound judgment eluded me when it came to Palmer. That was why I had to get the hell away from here as soon as this job was done.

But for now, fuck it. I was like a junkie on my way to get high. My whole body buzzed with sexual energy and my cock strained against my jeans, making me shift in my seat.

"Is it different when other women give you … oral sex?" Palmer asked. "Are they better at it than I was?"

Her earnest expression made me want to reach over and reassure her with a touch. But I kept my hands on the wheel.

"It's tough to explain," I said.

"It's okay, you can tell me. I'm sure experience is a good thing in that department."

Here was a chance to get a small dig in on her – to give back a tiny dose of the hurt she'd inflicted on me. But I couldn't lie.

"With other women, it's a means to an end. I just want to get off. I close my eyes and either clear my head or … think about you. With you, I loved to watch you doing it. I loved teaching you how I liked it. Knowing you'd never sucked off anyone but me was a huge turn-on."

She pressed a hand to her thigh and squeezed it, looking straight ahead at the road. "Just listening to you talk makes me so … We never used to talk about sex."

I couldn't help grinning. "That's true. We talked about when we were gonna do it, but never about sex itself."

"Where are we going?"

"To a lot I own close by."

"A vacant lot?" Palmer turned to me, eyes wide with alarm.

"It's more than a lot. It's several dozen acres of wooded area. I bought it from my dad's company when I started mine. It's very private."

In an effort to relax her, I turned on some music. She looked nervous, though I had no idea why. Palmer didn't even have to try to turn me on. Just being in her presence got me going.

I turned onto a dirt road that led into the woods, parking in front of a metal gate that blocked the path. The key to unlock it was in my glove box, and Palmer's eyes swam over me as I leaned over to get the keychain.

She looked so pretty and so ready that I couldn't help myself. I bent to her lap and pressed a kiss to her bare thigh, just below her skirt. Her body tightened and she moaned softly in her throat.

Having the upper hand felt so fucking good. I got out of the truck and walked to the gate, taking my time unlocking it. Drawing out her arousal would only heighten her pleasure when we reached that point.

I pulled through the gate and locked it behind us. This property was all woods – entirely secluded. I drove another quarter of a mile so Palmer would feel secure that no one could possibly see us here. When I parked the truck, she looked at me and licked her lips.

"Take your shirt off," I said. "And your bra."

She hesitated a second, but then did it. My pulse quickened as the red bra slid away, exposing her small, pert breasts. I wanted to reach out and touch them, but I knew where that would lead. I had something else in mind today.

I responded to her expectant gaze, seeing how much she liked me taking the lead.

"Take your panties off next. Leave the skirt on. And take your hair down."

When her long, soft hair tumbled around her bare shoulders, the ends brushing across her nipples, I groaned and forced my hands to remain still. Her soft white skin was begging to be caressed.

"Are you wet, Palmer?" I asked, my eyes locked on hers. She flushed and nodded. I put a hand on her knee and ran it up her inner thigh, her breath catching in her throat as I advanced beneath her skirt.

My fingers brushed over damp curls and I knew she was wet before I eased a finger inside her. Her eyes glazed with lust and I felt a rush of power from owning her in this moment. There was nothing but this – no tension, no worry, no sadness.

She reached for the fly of my jeans, fumbling to unbutton them. I pulled my hand back and helped her, her expression of need reaching something deep inside me. When my cock was freed from my boxers, Palmer pressed my hips, urging me to move my back against the door so she could bend over my lap.

Where was my innocent, skittish former fiancée? I'd never seen this side of her, and it was about to undo me before she even touched me.

I had to regain control, and I fought to as she bent and licked the head of my cock. She was so sexy and sweet at the same time. I wanted to just stroke my hands through her hair and watch. But our primal sex on her kitchen counter had cracked the door open to more.

"You teased me all morning, baby," I said, my voice gruff as I spoke through the arousal. "Walking around in that skirt giving me those looks. We're done with that now. Put my cock in your throat."

The hum of her moan as she descended down my shaft forced the breath out of me. She worked her mouth up and down my cock, her hands gripping my thighs.

I moved her hair aside so I could watch, and it was almost too much. It was so hard to hold back while she sucked me so eagerly, her eyes dark with desire. I wound a hand into her hair and flexed my hips forward.

"Fuck, that's hot," I said as she took me deep. As much as I wanted to stretch this out as long as I could, the sight of her ass in the air of my truck's front seat was too much. After another minute, I came hard, groaning and pulling on the hair my hand was entangled in. Her eyes stayed locked on mine, and I shuddered and let out a ragged exhale, overwhelmed by the intensity she brought out of me.

She swallowed every drop, and every muscle in my body relaxed. Even after all this time, she still had a deeper effect on me than any other woman ever had. The thought made my stomach stir uncomfortably.

"You like that?" I asked, regaining myself. I had to get back in control of this situation. "Let me taste myself on you."

Her lips parted with surprise and I seized the chance to kiss her, hard and deep. I'd never talked to her like this when we were together – it'd been all soft and lovey. But now there were no limits.

"I like that," I said, pulling away and reaching between her thighs. "You're such a sweet little cocksucker, baby. I taught you well."

As soon as my fingers brushed across her clit, her body tensed in response. But she relaxed a second later, sliding her hips back and forth to create friction.

"You wanna come?" I asked, locking eyes with her. She nodded, her face cloudy with desire. I considered drawing it out, but my fingers worked her instinctively, spreading the wetness over her swollen clit. A small, desperate sound escaped her lips as she got close, and I put my fingers just where she needed them.

"Come for me, Palmer. You like it this way, don't you? Getting fingered in my truck like a desperate, dirty girl."

She gripped my shoulders hard and cried out. I added more pressure, entranced with her lusty expression as she rode out her orgasm against my hand. When she relaxed the dig of her nails through my shirt, I slowed down, and she smiled shyly.

"That was so worth skipping lunch for," she said, sliding away and pulling her skirt down over her hips.

"If you're hungry we can grab a sandwich on the way back."

"Yeah."

I cleared my throat as I buttoned my jeans, glancing at her.

"Uh, I didn't mean to suggest sandwiches two seconds after you came. Did you want to …?"

She arched her brows and gave me the smile that could make me say yes to anything. "What, cuddle? We're in your truck, so I wasn't expecting it."

"Okay." I started the truck, resisting my urge to lean over and kiss her. The moment was over. We'd hooked up, gotten off and were done now. It was time to go back to work, where I could hopefully get her out of my head.

Palmer

When I pulled into Mom's driveway, I still had a smile on my face from my lunchtime escapade with Brady. During that time in his truck, I hadn't felt like a woman with the weight of the world on her shoulders. I'd felt young, carefree, and more than a little naughty.

I'd order pizza tonight. Danny and I would watch baseball and we'd have a slow evening at home. I was thinking about what I'd order when I spotted his wheelchair near the side entrance to the house – empty.

My heart flew into overdrive. I grabbed the door handle and threw my door open, panicked tears stinging my eyes.

"Danny!" I cried, running toward his chair. It was Mom I worried about, and I'd forgotten that Danny was also fragile and vulnerable.

I looked around the chair for any signs of what had happened. It just sat silently, offering no clues.

"Danny! Where are you?"

I fumbled through my purse for my cell phone, my head spinning. Why had I trusted my brother's care to a stranger? I wouldn't be able to live with myself if he was hurt.

Steadying my shaking hand, I was about to dial 911 when a note of high-pitched laughter made me turn toward the small backyard. I ran toward it, still feeling like I was about to jump out of my skin when I rounded the corner.

It was Amanda laughing, a wide grin on her face as she walked behind Danny, holding on to a belt around his waist. He was leaning his weight on a walker, taking tiny steps with his good foot and dragging the other one behind him. A radio broadcast of a baseball game was playing on an old radio from atop Mom's broken down picnic table.

"You got this, rockstar," Amanda said to Danny. His expression was the same one of tight-lipped determination I'd seen when he wheeled his own chair. "Back to your chair, Danny. You can do this."

When Danny looked up and saw me, my tears ran over. Not just from relief, but also the look of sheer pride on his face.

"Danny," I said softly. I approached and cupped his cheeks in my hands.

"Almer," he said, glowing. For the first time ever, my little brother was taller than me. He smiled down at me and I forced myself not to burst into a full-on sob.

"I'll get your chair," I said, turning. I gave Amanda a murderous glance, but she didn't look the least bit surprised by it.

"He doesn't need it," she said. "He's gonna walk to it. Let him do this, Palmer."

My heart pounded, now with outrage rather than worry. How dare this woman raise my brother's hopes?

"His doctor said a long time ago that a wheelchair was the best option for Danny," I said, forcing my voice to stay pleasant.

"I think it is, in some circumstances. But this is good for him, too. With physical therapy, I think he could do things that would surprise you."

I stood back, offended and rebuffed at the same time. "He's my brother. I know what's best for him."

As soon as the words left my mouth, I heard my mother's voice arguing with the professionals who'd worked with Danny over the years. *'He's my son. I know what's best for him.'*

So she'd kept him at her side, seeing to his every need. Danny had never been pushed because Mom was always worried he'd get hurt or disappointed.

"Trust me, Palmer," Amanda said, meeting my gaze with a warm smile. "Encourage him and praise him and he will make it to that chair."

I nodded, tears clouding my vision as Danny started his slow trip toward me.

"Danny," I said, smiling widely in hopes that my tears wouldn't confuse him. "You're amazing. You're doing so great. Take your time."

After a few steps, he stopped, breathing more heavily than usual. I looked questioningly at Amanda. She clutched the stretchy support belt in one hand and rubbed a hand over his back with the other.

"Deep breaths, Danny. This is hard work," she said in a soothing tone.

Soon, he resumed his step and shuffle rhythm. When he rounded the corner and his chair came into view, he gave a whoop of happiness.

"Okay, Palmer," Amanda said. "Go to the chair and turn it so we can help him sit down without him needing to turn."

I went to the chair and turned it, waiting.

"What would you have done if I wasn't here?" I asked, my protective instincts still not fully convinced this was a good idea.

"We use the house to support the chair," she said.

"You've done this before?" I closed my eyes, chiding myself for my judgmental tone. "What I mean is, you've done this before! Danny, I am so proud of you!"

Sweat trickled down his temple as he made the final few steps. I took one elbow and Amanda took the other. We helped him ease into his chair, where he waved his arms around and cried out happily.

I reached for him and hugged him close, a fresh round of tears spilling over.

"That was amazing. I love you, Danny. You make me so proud."

I kissed his cheek and pulled back, and Amanda held her fist out for a bump.

"Great job," she said. "I'm proud of you, too. Now we'll go in so you can watch the rest of this game on TV."

"You want to stay for pizza?" I asked her.

"Sure, thanks."

She started to wheel Danny up the ramp to the door, glancing at me as I reached for the door handle.

"Hey," she said. "There's someone from hospice in with your mom. I called them because she was having pain. I think she's resting comfortably now, but the nurse is just making sure everything's good before she goes."

I swallowed and nodded. I'd met the hospice representatives recently and then put them out of my mind as soon as they were out the door. The things they talked about were just too painful to consider. But now there was no choice.

"I'd like to go in and see her," I said. "Can you call the pizza place on the magnet on the fridge and order? I'm not picky. Danny just doesn't like green peppers."

Amanda nodded. As soon as we got Danny's chair in, I took a deep breath and headed for the door to Mom's tiny bedroom.

I pushed the door open and saw a woman sitting in a kitchen chair next to the bed, reading on a glowing e-reader. The curtains were drawn and a fan was whirring in the corner of the room.

"Hi," she whispered, standing. "I'm Sara."

"Palmer," I said. "Her daughter."

"Very nice to meet you. She's doing much better now. The medicine works quickly."

My face crumpled as I willed myself not to cry.

"I feel bad that I wasn't here," I said. "I wish Amanda had called me."

Sara wrapped her plump hand around mine. "She was just having some pain. That'll happen and it's what we're here for. She's okay now – just resting."

Mom's withered, frail form, motionless in the bed, reminded me that one day soon, she wouldn't be okay.

"She'll wake up, right?" I asked.

"Yes, but not for quite a while."

I nodded and wrapped my arms around myself. "Good. I want to tell her about Danny walking. She'll be so happy to hear about it."

The words brought on more tears. There were so many moments to come that Mom wouldn't be part of. Sara wrapped me up in a hug, rocking me slightly as I cried in her shirt.

I pulled away after a few minutes, wiping my face. "I'm sorry. You meet me one minute and I'm getting your shirt snotty the next."

She waved a hand. "This is what I'm here for. I'll just sit with her for a little while longer."

"Thanks."

I left the bedroom and darted into the bathroom, needing a moment alone before I rejoined Danny and Amanda. My high from Danny's accomplishment had dropped to a scary new low in a matter of seconds.

And things would get even lower. The thought made me crave Brady. All I wanted in this moment was the escape that only he could give me. To have no room for anything but the anticipation of his next touch and the satisfaction it always brought.

But that wasn't an option right now. I picked up a washcloth and wet it, wiping the smeared eye makeup from my face. Tonight I was going to eat pizza and spend time with Danny. But hopefully tomorrow I'd get to see Brady again.

Chapter 10

Palmer

There was no one in sight when I parked my car on the gravel road at Derek and Adriane's house and stepped out. The place was usually buzzing with at least three dozen workers.

I realized when I saw the trucks parked in their usual spots that the guys were here, but on lunch break. The picnic tables were set up on the other side of Brady's trailer, where I couldn't see them.

Damn. Georges and I couldn't make out one of the kitchen measurements on our set of plans, and I'd eagerly jumped in the car to come over here and get it. Or maybe it was more like desperately. No matter. I was here, and Brady wasn't.

With a sigh, I carefully made my way through the gravel and into the house. The framing was substantially complete now, and the house was taking shape. It was going to be incredible.

I got my measurement and was about to leave the empty kitchen when I heard footsteps approaching.

"Hey," Brady said.

"Hi." I tried to keep it casual, but my heart was beating in overdrive. He wore a gray t-shirt with the sleeves ripped off, a good match for his jeans with a giant rip in one knee.

"You like keeping me in a constant state of arousal?"

His accusing tone caught me off-guard. I'd thought that was what we were playing at here.

"I can't say I dislike it," I said. "But really I'm just working, Brady. You act like I'm doing a striptease or something."

He approached me, coming so close I felt the heat of his body.

"If you walk in here wearing heels and a skirt and a sleeveless shirt, I'm considering it code that you want me to fuck you."

A thread of arousal sparked between my thighs and spread to the rest of me, warming my skin. I breathed out through my parted lips and tucked my hair behind one ear.

"Okay," I said softly, mentally calculating how many sleeveless shirts I had in my closet. "The skirt I get, and the heels, but I didn't realize sleeveless shirts did it for you."

"On you they do. You have beautiful shoulders. Such soft, perfect skin. Seeing them makes me think of holding on to them while I fuck you from behind."

His gaze licked across my skin like the flames of a fire. The hunger in his eyes gave me a more delicious thrill than being touched would have. It was so much deeper than the gaze of a stranger. He knew my body – knew every inch of me. The image of him behind me, pounding me, made my skin warm all over. We'd never done it that way before, but I wanted it in a bad way right now.

"You want me?" he asked, his voice so low it was almost a whisper. "You wanna go out in my truck and get fucked hard for teasing me?"

"Yes." I wanted it more than I'd ever thought possible, and I wanted it now.

He nodded. "Can you meet me here at two?"

I nodded, unable to speak.

"Be ready for some payback, baby. I can't focus on work when my dick's hard."

He wasn't the only one who couldn't focus. I tried to think about work, but my physical ache for Brady overrode all other thoughts. He saw through everything else to the woman who was still buried deep inside me. Past my roles as caregiver and comforter, provider and business owner.

Brady still found me sexy, and the feeling was like a life preserver in the storm my life felt like these days.

I was more than ready, waiting by his truck when he approached just before two, pulling on a clean t-shirt as he walked.

His body was my ultimate aphrodisiac. I knew what those ridged muscles felt like beneath my fingertips; knew the highs he could bring me to with those hips and the hard shaft that was the only one I'd ever known.

"How are you?" he asked, glancing at me as he opened the passenger door for me.

"I'm good. How 'bout you?"

"Great. Ready for this lunch. I'm starving."

I hoped he didn't mean food, but when his eyes darkened just before he closed the door, I knew we were on the same page.

We made small talk about the house, and it felt like a conversation with any other contractor until we got close to the undeveloped wooded lot and Brady looked over at my bare thighs.

"Pull up the skirt so I can look at you," he said.

"Right here?" He was pulling up to a red light and I looked out the window at the car next to us.

"No one but me can see, Palmer."

He wanted it, which made me want to do it. I worked the skirt up over my hips, exposing my black panties. Brady watched, not looking away until the car behind him honked that the light was green.

"You drive me crazy," he said, turning his gaze back to the road. "I think about you before bed every fucking night. You're the subject of every sexual fantasy I have."

His words brought on the powerful, sexy feeling that no one else could bring out of me.

"I want you so bad," I said. "I'm aching to have you inside me."

He put a hand on his crotch, rubbing his bulge and stepping on the truck's accelerator.

"Turn toward me so I can see you," he said. I complied, turning my hips and feeling myself get wet as he looked between my thighs, eyes glazed.

We'd gotten to the wooded lot, and he jumped from the truck to unlock the gate, not bothering to re-lock it. He drove to the same spot as last time, parking and reaching into the back seat.

"Back of the truck," he said shortly, pulling out a brown canvas coat. I got out and walked around to the back, where Brady opened the tailgate and stepped up into the bed.

He bent down and wrapped his hands around my waist, exposed since my skirt was hiked up, lifting me into the truck. It was all I could do to wait the two seconds it took him to toss his work coat on the bed of the truck.

"Hand and knees," he commanded, and I dropped to my knees on the coat, grateful for something soft. My elbows had barely touched the bed of the truck when I felt Brady yanking down my panties.

I heard the rip of a condom package, and within a few seconds, he was inside me, our moans and groans the only sounds in the silent forest. He pumped his hips hard, and I knew I wouldn't last long. Given what we were doing, I didn't even feel shameless when I reached between my thighs and stroked myself, saying his name as I climbed close to release.

He grabbed one of my shoulders, pounding harder and going deeper, and I couldn't hold on any longer. I came violently, pressing my face to his coat to muffle my screams.

Just a second later, he came with one last, violent thrust. "Shit," he said, his voice strained. "Palmer."

He sat down, breathless. I curled up next to him in the fetal position, my body humming from the hard, satisfying sex.

How had I lived a day to day life without thinking of him every second? I couldn't imagine managing that for nearly a year, and I knew that when he left this time, it would be impossible.

Margie Hillenbrand ran her heavily jeweled fingers over the wood cabinet samples on a table in my office.

"I just don't know," she said, frowning. "I like the dark wood a lot. But I like the light one, too."

"Everything else is so neutral that you can choose either and it'll look good," I said. "Do you want to take these home and look at them in the kitchen to see if that helps?"

"I don't know. Will that help, or just make me more indecisive?"

Margie was notoriously unable to make decisions. It was why I'd had to hire a crew to paint her master bedroom beige – no, green – no, beige. Money wasn't an object for her, but still I hated to see clients spend unnecessary money.

"It's just such a big decision," she said, rubbing her forehead.

"It is," I agreed. "You take these home and look at them in all lights. Ask your husband what he thinks. And if you need me to, I'll bring in a full size cabinet in each color once we get the room painted to see if that helps."

Her brows arched hopefully. "You could do that?"

"Absolutely. It would add a couple weeks to the project, because these are special order and our plan was to order them now. But we want to know you're getting exactly what you want."

She nodded and picked up the samples. "Thanks, Palmer. I'll call you in a few days."

We said goodbye and I grabbed my phone and sank into my office chair. For the fifteenth time, I read the text Brady had sent me this morning.

Brady: Come to the house this morning. No panties. I'll be checking.

My body had warmed in an instant when I read it, and the sensation hadn't gone away. I'd focused on work, but in the back of my mind I'd been fantasizing about Brady's dark eyes taking me in from head to toe, and just how he planned to do the promised checking.

"I have to run out," I said to Georges. "Be back this afternoon."

He was so immersed in his laptop that he just grunted. I was glad I'd avoided questions, because he knew I had no legitimate reason to go to Derek and Adriane's house today.

I slipped into the bathroom, a shiver of arousal coursing through me as I slid my panties off and stuffed them into my purse. I'd never worn skirts daily, but knowing how Brady felt about them had made them my go-to wardrobe choice.

It was an odd feeling, having no panties on as I drove my car. I kept my thighs clenched together the whole way, my nervous excitement escalating as I got closer.

When I parked and slipped into the house, I barely drew anyone's notice. Hunter gave me a quick wave from his spot atop scaffolding, but no one else said a word.

"You free for an early lunch?" Brady asked from behind me.

I turned and nodded, wanting to blurt out that I wasn't wearing panties. I managed to hold back, and Brady led the way to his truck silently.

As soon as we pulled onto the main road, he looked over and spoke in a low, commanding tone.

"Show me."

I didn't even consider not doing it this time. I pulled my skirt up around my hips, never looking away from him.

"Dammit, I'm liable to wreck the truck," he muttered. "How can I keep my eyes on the road now?"

I'd skipped lunch yesterday to get a bikini wax. An overdue one, since I'd been the only one who'd seen that area for a long time.

I turned my hips toward him on my own this time, parting my thighs wide so he could get a good look.

"You like?" I asked.

"I love," he said, giving me a serious glance. "I love your pussy, Palmer. It's absolutely perfect."

I flushed at the compliment, desperate to get to our rendezvous point and feel him inside me.

"Put your finger inside," he said.

I hesitated, feeling self-conscious. This was already more brazen than anything I'd ever considered.

"Come on." Brady urged me on in a gravely tone. "Give me what I want, baby."

And I did. While he waited at a red light, I slipped a finger in, sighing softly.

"Let me taste," he said.

"Brady ... I don't—"

"Put your finger in my mouth, Palmer."

It was pointless to even consider refusing. Nothing got me off like pleasing him. I slipped my finger between his lips, my pulse escalating as he sucked on it, running his tongue over my wet fingertip.

God, it was taking a long time to get to our spot today. I was so ready to have the hard, mind blowing sex Brady gave me every time.

"You taste so good," he murmured when I pulled my finger out, tracing it over his bottom lip.

"I'm so ... hot right now. You can make me that way in a matter of seconds, you know."

He glanced at me, a smile playing on his lips. "I do know. It's the one thing I have control of with us. You've got me in every other area."

"I don't know about that."

"It's true. I'd walk through fire for you."

His tone had a sliver of resentment, and I was about to ask him about it when he signaled and pulled into a familiar drive.

"Wait," I said. "What? We're back at Derek and Adriane's."

Brady gave me a smug smile. "So we are. Back to work."

I grabbed my skirt, frantically pulling it down to cover myself.

"What the hell, Brady? You texted me and drove me around and got me all hot and bothered just to tease me?"

He shrugged. "Thought I deserved a turn. You come in here teasing me with those skirts and those 'fuck me' looks all the time."

I glared at him, sneaking a glance at his lap. "Well, what's your plan for the situation in your pants? You gonna work like that?"

"Hell no. I'm going to my trailer to think about you and jerk off."

I folded my arms across my chest as the truck slowed. "Well, that makes a hell of a lot of sense."

"Just building your appetite, sweetheart. It'll make the sex better on Friday night."

I bit back a comment about not wanting to see him Friday night, because I'd regret that. He put the car in park and I gave him a dirty look as I opened my door.

"Have a nice time masturbating, asshole. I'm going back to the office."

His brows quirked up with amusement. "You're sexy when you're angry."

I rolled my eyes and got out of the truck. "See you Friday," I called behind me. "Unless you change your mind again."

"No, Friday's on," he answered. "Hey, hold on."

I stopped, not looking back as he jogged the few steps between us. He stood in front of me, cupping one of my cheeks in his large palm.

"Hey. You're not really pissed at me, are you?"

"No," I said in a sulky tone. "Just frustrated."

"I'll make it up to you Friday night." He wrapped his other palm around my hip, pulled me to him and kissed me.

It took my breath away. Not just the kiss, but the fact that he'd run to me for it, not caring who saw.

"See you then," I whispered. He kissed me one more time before nodding and turning, the teasing whoops and hollers from his crew starting up immediately.

That man. Even with his ability to frustrate the hell out of me, he'd become my port in the storm.

Brady

Palmer was losing her fight to keep her eyes open, and it wasn't even 9 pm. We'd gone out for dinner and been on each other the second we walked in her front door afterwards. But after one round of sex, she was about to fall asleep next to me.

I'd been looking forward to Friday night with her all week. This was the only time she really relaxed. And damn, was she relaxed right now. Her hair was loose around her shoulders. Her long, bare thigh was wound around my leg, and I ran my fingertips down her satin skin.

Her eyes fluttered open and met mine. She smiled and reached for my cheek, running her fingertips over my unshaven skin.

"Sorry I'm so tired," she said softly.

"It's alright. You want me to go so you can sleep?"

"No. I'll get a second wind. Mom wanted to look at old photo albums last night, and we were up really late."

She was the most beautiful thing I'd ever seen. The hallways lights cast a glow over her as she lay on her side looking at me. I ran a hand down her hip, bittersweet memories invading my peace. I'd thought this was how we'd start and end every day – together, tousled and connecting in the most intimate ways.

"Baby pictures of you?" I said, forcing away thoughts of what was supposed to be. "I never saw any of those when we were together. Were you cute?"

"Aren't all babies cute?"

"No. I've seen some unfortunate looking ones."

She laughed, the sound filling me with warmth.

"How's Colorado?" she asked, surprising me with the quick subject change. "I mean, really. Are you happy there?"

As much as I wanted to, I didn't let the truth slip out.

"Yeah. It's good. Business is great there. The hunting and fishing's great, too."

"Is that what you do on weekends?"

I shrugged. "When I can. I work a lot of weekends."

"Do you miss your dad?"

I furrowed my brow and considered. "Yeah. And I worry about my mom all alone. Wonder if she gets lonely, you know?"

She moved the leg she had wrapped around mine, her toes tracing a line down my calf. "Do you get lonely?"

I fought my urge to tell her the truth – that I did, and it wasn't supposed to be this way. But pride stopped me. I didn't want her to know that even after all this time, I still missed her.

"No time to get lonely," I said. "I'm too damned busy. Probably a lot like you."

Her lips curled into a soft smile. "I get lonely," she said, her eyelids looking heavy again.

"You lonely right now?" I traced a path down her hip again, her smooth skin and the sweet scent of her perfume making me wish for Round Two.

"No. I'm never lonely when I'm with you."

Her eyes dropped closed and within a few seconds her even breathing told me she was asleep. I studied her face in the pale light. So gorgeous, and while her beauty had a delicacy, I knew there was tenacious strength beneath.

Even though she'd knocked me on my ass, Palmer was still my dream. I turned to my back, staring up at the ceiling I'd planned to scrape and re-plaster after we got married.

I had to get out of here. Only an asshole would stay and lap up more crumbs in the morning. I slid out of bed gently, finding my jeans and pulling them on. I took my shirt and boots into the living room and put them on. Then I left, locking the door on my way out.

Our Friday night fuck was over. I needed to move on with my weekend.

Chapter 11

Palmer

Today's black skirt, red heels and sleeveless shirt had been chosen just for Brady. I smiled sweetly at him as I walked by the spot where he was framing with his crew in the hot summer sun, his sweaty shirt hanging from his back pocket.

His eyes followed my every step, and I felt a thrill I could hardly contain. Georges snickered next to me.

"His tongue is practically on the ground," he murmured, amused.

I looked right at Brady and licked my lips. I may not have been a vixen, but I knew how to get his attention. At the sound of a catcall from the one of the other guys, he lowered his brows and turned.

Georges and I headed for the basement, and I relaxed since I was out of Brady's line of sight now.

"Did you see that guy with the tats?" Georges said, biting his lip. "This place is Testosterone Central."

I shook my head. "I don't notice anyone but Brady."

"Obviously, you guys are still getting it on?"

"Yeah, but it's tough with my schedule."

"Just a Friday night thing, then?"

I avoided Georges' inquiring gaze. "Yeah, and ... lunch hour."

He gasped and arched his brows. "Nice. I didn't know you had it in you, Palmer."

"Neither did I. Now let's get out our flooring samples and color inspirations."

We unpacked swatches and paint samples from our bags. Georges moved them to different spots in the room, gauging the natural light.

"I emailed Adriane the furniture we like for this room and she signed off on everything," I said, making a note in my sketchpad.

"Even my zebra print chaise?" Georges eyed me hopefully.

"Yep. She loved it all."

We worked in silence, nearly finished with our to-do list when the sound of heavy work boots pounding on the stairs to the basement made me turn. My heart was thudding as loud as those boots because I knew whose they were.

"Hey, George," he said, nodding.

"It's *Georges.*"

My business partner had changed the pronunciation of his name a couple of years ago, but Brady had never gotten on board, having known him since he was George Brammer.

"Palmer, can I talk to you?" Brady asked. Georges coughed theatrically and I shot him a dirty look.

"Sure." I set down my supplies and walked over to him, his eyes locked on me. When he turned to walk up the stairs, though, it was my gaze that wouldn't be moved. He was still shirtless, the muscles of his back and biceps defined and sweaty. I wanted to reach out at touch him, but I reminded myself of my humiliation when he'd left me panting for him in the front seat of his truck.

"In my trailer?" he asked, glancing at me over his shoulder. Oh, so *now* he was in the mood.

"Why can't we just talk right here?"

"'Cause I'm thirsty, and I've got water in the trailer," he said shortly. "Plus it's air-conditioned."

"Fine," I said, a little sharper than I meant to. Any illusions I had about playing hard to get went out the window. I was about to be alone with the sweaty, sexy man I'd spread my legs for in broad daylight. In his truck, no less.

He slowed his pace so I could fall into step next to him.

"You look very nice today," he said, arching his brows and grinning.

"You think so? Thank you."

He shook his head and looked ahead at the trailer. "Ah, Palmer. What you need is a few nice, hard smacks on your ass."

My inner thighs clenched together in agreement. "If only I knew someone who could perform such a service," I said lightly.

We'd reached the trailer, and he opened the door and waited while I walked in. He was on my heels, and he scooped me into his arms as soon as the door latch closed.

"Damn, I don't wanna get you all sweaty," he said, easing back a little.

"You had me all sweaty before you even touched me," I said, pressing myself against him.

He groaned and wound a hand into my hair, pulling me in for a kiss. His fresh wood smell mingled with the salty, sweaty taste of him, and I couldn't get enough.

"Oh," a male voice said, surprised. "Sorry, man. I was just takin' a piss."

We both turned and saw Troy coming out of the bathroom, averting his eyes from us.

"Get the fuck outta here," Brady said gruffly. Troy hurried out the door and Brady pulled the door to a small refrigerator open. He took out two bottles of water and handed me one.

"I'm going home Tuesday," he said. "My crew there started a big commercial reno and I need to be on site."

My stomach dropped with trepidation. "Oh. Does that mean you won't be coming back here?"

He cocked a brow at me and grinned. "Worried about losing your fuck buddy? I'm gonna travel back and forth for the next couple months."

I glared at him and crossed my arms over my chest. "You're not my fuck buddy."

He scoffed and shook his head. "Sorry sweetheart, but we get together and do nothing but fuck. That makes us fuck buddies."

His casual indifference made tears burn in my eyes, but I swallowed past the lump in my throat.

"Speak for yourself," I said. "You're a lot more than that to me."

Brady grabbed his neck and gave me an aggravated stare. "We were more than that to each other, but that's over. You called off our wedding and said you didn't need me, remember? And now you want me to say I'm still in love with you?"

"I didn't say that. But don't tell me I'm nothing but a fuck buddy. That hurts, Brady."

He grunted his dismissal of my words. "We're good at hurting each other, aren't we? Nothing's ever ripped me apart like you saying you didn't need me. My dad was the most important person in my life until I met you. And then you both let me down."

My anger boiled to the surface immediately. I edged closer to him, looking up to meet his eyes. "My mom was diagnosed with a terminal illness, you asshole."

"Exactly. Just when you should've needed me most, you told me to fuck off."

"No, you took it that way, Brady. I wanted to postpone the wedding."

He shook his head with disgust. "You told me to go to Colorado, Palmer! Told me to start fresh. How the fuck is that not dumping me?"

"I wanted what was best for you!"

He bent, his green eyes swimming with emotion as his face drew closer to mine. "*You* were best for me, Palmer. I wanted you above all else. More than I wanted to start my own company or get the hell away from my father. But you didn't give me any choice."

The pain I'd buried inside me a year ago was rising to the surface, my anger lowering my defenses.

"You say that, Brady, but you don't know. You don't understand. It wasn't just about your business."

"Then what?" he demanded. "If we meant something to each other, and if I still mean something to you, have the fuckin' guts to be honest with me."

The words flew from my mouth, uncensored by my better judgment. "Danny, alright? It was because of Danny, Brady."

He drew back, confusion lining his face. "What's Danny got to do with any of this?"

"My mom has taken care of him since he was born. Who do you think will do that when she's gone? I have a hard time even working and taking care of him. There's nothing left of me. No vacations, no nights out and no children of my own. Is that what you want in a wife?"

I stepped forward, propelled by the rage that had welled inside me for so long, and Brady took a step back. His look of pure shock told me none of this had ever crossed his mind. Now that I'd started, I couldn't stop.

"You accused me of cheating on you! How'd that feel, Brady? Did it make you feel like a big, bad asshole to kick me when I was already down? And the truth is I didn't want to burden you with the lifelong commitment of caring for a disabled person."

"Palmer, I love Danny."

I stomped my foot, wishing I could lash out and punch him right now. "This is different. You don't understand. Danny is my blood and I would die for him. But taking care of him around the clock is so goddamn hard. It pushes me to the limit."

Brady's expression wasn't angry; he stared at me with disbelief, which was worse.

"I would've stayed. If you'd been honest with me, I would've stayed. I can't fucking believe you didn't want my help. That was it? This whole time? You thought I'd be pissed about not being able to take vacations?"

"It's not just that! We both wanted children. I can't take care of kids and my brother."

"I could've hired help, Palmer. I've got the money."

"Yeah, you do now. *Because you went to Colorado.* If you had stayed, you'd have been a hand on someone else's crew, and we wouldn't have been able to afford help."

Brady ran a hand through his hair and glared at me, his anger resurging. "We would've figured it out. My mom would've helped. The fucking point is, you made all these decisions alone. You didn't love me enough to be honest with me and get through it together."

I couldn't hold back anymore. When I advanced and punched him in the shoulder, he didn't even move. "It was because I loved you! I wanted you to have a chance at a normal life! I knew you would've stayed, and you might've regretted it."

I panted, exerted from the screaming and punching. Brady locked his hands around my wrists, holding my hands in place against his chest.

"You're so fucking wrong about me, Palmer. I didn't think you could cut me any deeper, but you just did. I was ready for better or worse when I proposed. And you think I'm a self-serving asshole who resents putting others first."

He squeezed my wrists and flung them away from his chest. His eyes weren't blazing with fury anymore. There was just a flat, resigned detachment. When he turned for the door, my anger boiled over again.

"Yeah, go," I said. "That's what you do when things get hard."

He stopped and shook his head, but didn't turn around. "You pushed me here. You seem to want it to prove you can do it all alone. Guess you got what you wanted."

When the door closed this time, I just stared at it, too stunned to cry. That wouldn't last, though. I had to find the courage to walk out of here and get back to my car before breaking down.

I let my anger rise back up to the surface as I left the trailer, forcing an indifferent expression. Damned if I'd let Brady *and* his crew see me cry. I pulled out my phone and texted Georges to meet me in the car. It was too bad the only man who really had my back didn't like women.

We'd almost made it back to the office by the time I finished pouring the whole story out to Georges.

"Don't agree with me just because you're my best friend," I said. "Be honest. Am I right or wrong?"

Georges cocked his head, considering. "Both. But you're slightly more wrong than he is."

"How so?" I demanded.

"You should've told him why from the beginning."

I groaned and gripped the steering wheel as hard as I could. "You know why I didn't."

"Yeah, and I call bullshit. Have you forgotten that I'm the one who set you up with Brady? I actually knew him. It wasn't just his looks that made me think he was good enough for my best friend."

"I never would've known if he really wanted to stay," I said, my frustration near the boiling point.

"Yeah, but he never even got a chance to decide. Not fair. He was so in love with you."

The word *was* made my heart sink.

"Fine," I agreed. "Maybe I should have told him. But how was he wrong?"

"He should forgive you for it. Maybe he just needs time to process it."

I sighed deeply, parking my car in my space at the deck by our office and resting my head on the steering wheel.

"I can't do this right now. I'm so stressed out. I'm spread so emotionally thin already that I just … can't deal with it."

"He chose a very shitty time to get into it with you," Georges agreed.

"And to rub my face in my alone-ness. Like I need to be reminded."

"I'm not dark and sexy, but you've got me," Georges said, rubbing his palm over my back. "You aren't alone."

I turned my head to look at him. "I love you."

"Love you, too. Now let's go listen to the Indigo Girls and eat the chocolates stashed in my desk."

Brady

The sheet rock crew worked silently, most of them wearing headphones and listening to music. I envied those guys today. I wanted to be alone with my thoughts. Instead I had to meet with subcontractors about upcoming deadlines.

I put my Grant Brothers Builders hat on, about to head to my truck when Palmer's business partner stomped into the future great room of Derek's house, wearing perfectly pressed khakis and a pissed off scowl.

"George," I said with a nod.

"It's *Georges*," he corrected, tapping a foot on the floor.

"When I was an advisor for your college Construction Fundamentals class, you were George Brammer. So I'm callin' you George."

"That's because you're an asshole," he said, advancing toward me. I had to give the guy credit. I had about seven inches and fifty pounds on him, but there was no fear on his face.

"So I've heard," I said, taking the hat off and running a hand through my hair.

"Why did I ever introduce you to Palmer? You've broken her heart time and again."

I pulled the hat down snug and glared at him. "All right, *Georges*. Time for you to fuck off."

He crossed his arms and shook his head. "No. You may be able to walk out on her, but I will not *let* you walk out on me."

At the sound of muffled laughter from two of my guys on the other side of the room, I scowled at him.

"I'm serious. I'm working, and I'm not in the mood for your shit."

"How dare you let her down when she needs you most?"

I pointed a finger at him and covered the distance between us. "Fuck you. You have no idea what happened. She was the one who called off the wedding, not me. If I'd had my way, she'd be my wife right now."

"I don't mean back then." He narrowed his eyes at me. "I mean *right now*. Her mother is dying. Not just diagnosed with a terminal illness, but actually near the end. She trusted you with the truth and you got pissed off and left her. *Again*."

"It was mutual," I snapped.

"Yeah, tell yourself that. I know what I've seen since the day she first saw you on this job. You reeled her back in with sex and made her think you still have feelings for her. And then as soon as you saw an opportunity to hurt her, you took it."

"No." I shook my head emphatically. "I didn't do that."

"You sure as hell did. I don't give a shit what she says or does right now, she is on the edge. She could tell me I'm a bitch from hell with no design talent whatsoever and I would hug her and tell her I love her. She is in so much pain. I will love her through this, no matter what. But you—" He stuck his index finger in my face. "You just see it as a chance to avenge your damaged pride."

I opened my mouth to respond, but closed it after a second. My head was spinning. Was he right? Had I taken advantage of Palmer? Just the thought made a sick knot form in my stomach. I never would've consciously done it.

"If you hurt her again, I will hurt you," Georges said, his face flushed with anger. "Don't doubt that I can. She is like family to me."

"I've got it," I said, nodding numbly. He spun around and left, but I stayed rooted to my spot on the subfloor. I felt sick to my stomach. My desire to control her, to own her, had clouded my judgment. It reminded me of my father – selfish and too fucking stubborn to even realize it.

Chapter 12

Brady

A woman in cutoffs and a tank top walked out of the visitor's entrance of the prison, cigarette in one hand, lighter in the other. The movement shook me out of my daze. I needed to either get out of my truck and go inside or get the hell out of here.

Going in won out – but barely. I headed for the front entrance, ignoring the smoking woman's open appraisal of me.

I went through the visitor's check-in motions, signing forms and passing through a metal detector before sitting down in a plastic orange chair to wait my turn. Mom wanted me to come see him. That was why I was here. Not because he deserved it.

When a guard let me into the visitor's room, I saw Dad sitting at a table alone, waiting. His hair was more salt than pepper now, and his face was leaner. When he looked up and saw me, his eyes softened and he broke out in a grin, standing and opening his arms for a hug.

He clapped me on the back and then stood back, looking me over.

"You look good," he said, his eyes glistening. "How are you?"

"No complaints. You?"

He shrugged. "I'm okay."

"How much longer you gonna be in here?"

"I'm eligible for release in nine months."

It didn't seem like much of a price to pay for the harm he'd inflicted. I arched my brows skeptically.

"So what then?"

He took a deep breath before answering. "I don't know. Depends what I'll be allowed to do work-wise on parole."

"Surely nothing that involves stewardship of other people's money," I muttered.

The corners of Dad's eyes wrinkled as he smiled slightly. "The thing about this, Brady, is that no one won."

"That's for damned sure. But the people whose money you stole lost at your hands."

He shook his head with frustration. "I have to make restitution."

"How?" I glared at him. "You gonna do enough odd jobs to make three hundred grand?"

"Let's not do this. It's been a year since we saw each other."

"Yeah. Well, I haven't been back home at all. Work's been busy in Colorado."

"That's good." He glanced at the closed door to the room. "Did Troy come with you?"

"No. I didn't tell him I was coming."

His face fell. "I haven't seen him since I've been in here. Can't he make time since he's close by?"

"That's up to him, I guess."

"You keeping him in line?"

I sighed, frustrated. "Doing my best."

"Stay on top of him." Dad leveled his gaze at me seriously. "He's been in trouble with some bad people. I'm up at night worrying about him."

Frustration welled in my chest, the pressure forcing me to shift in my seat. I didn't want to be here. It was impossible to make small talk with my father inside the prison where he was doing time.

"Promise me you'll look after him," Dad said earnestly.

I furrowed my brow and leaned forward on my elbows. "Are you fuckin' serious? You want me to promise I'll be the father figure you can't be from inside a cell? How 'bout this — promise *me* you haven't lied about anything else. Is Mom right to be waiting on you? Were you spending the money on other women?"

He paled, his lips set in a thin line. "Never, ever accuse me of cheating on your mother. She is my whole world. I lost my way because I wanted to be deserving of her."

I shook my head with disgust. "She deserves to not be alone right now. And don't bullshit me. Mom's not about material things. You made a good living and had a good life 'til you fucked it up trying to be a rich guy."

Dad sighed softly and gave me a look that was damn close to pity. "You don't see, do you? It wasn't about buying things. It was about Troy. He was deep in debt from drugs and gambling. He came to your mom and me crying – begging us for help. She was beside herself. Said we had to find a way. That she wouldn't be able to live with herself if anything happened to him."

My anger evaporated, replaced by a numb sense of disbelief.

"What?" I said, my voice raw. "How much money?"

"It was several debts to different people. He borrowed from one to pay off another, and with interest ... it took almost a hundred grand to clear it all up."

"Fuck." I ran a hand through my hair, my head spinning.

"I didn't have that much liquid cash, so I ... did what I did. I planned to pay it back, but then Troy was back the next week needing more. I kept it between me and him at that point, because I didn't want to worry your mother."

"So he knows," I said bitterly. "He knows damn well he's the reason you're here."

Dad held a hand up to stop me. "*I'm* the reason I'm here. I didn't have to do what I did. And I'm not telling you to create problems between you and Troy, I just can't stand you looking at me that way any longer. I've worried I'd die in here and you'd never know the truth. What I did was wrong, but I didn't see any other options at the time."

I studied the lines on his face, feeling like the worst kind of asshole.

"Dad, I still loved you," I said, clearing my throat. "Even when I thought you had no legitimate reason, I still loved you. I felt conflicted about admiring you, but there's nothing you could do to make me stop loving you."

He put a hand over his eyes, his shoulders shaking slightly.

"I never thought I'd hear either of my sons say those words to me again," he said softly.

"I wish you'd told me. The things people should say to each other but don't can be more toxic than the cruelest of words."

An image of Palmer flashed before my eyes. She was sitting at her kitchen table, overwrought with pain and worry. And I'd kicked her when she was down. Had I done the same to my father?

He wiped the corners of his eyes and smiled slightly. "That might be the most insightful thing anyone's ever said to me. I just didn't want anyone blaming Troy. It felt easier for you guys to be upset with me."

My brows shot up. "You guys? Mom doesn't know?"

He shrugged and sat back in his chair, folding his arms across his chest. "I'm sure she suspects, knowing Troy was in trouble with money. I told her he was taken care of – that I'd never let anything bad happen to him, and she didn't ask any other questions."

I swallowed hard, the image of Palmer still in front of me.

"Dad, something similar happened with me and Palmer. We broke up because her mom's terminally ill, and she didn't want me to be burdened with taking care of her brother."

A light of recognition dawned on his face. "He has cerebral palsy, right?"

"Yeah. But he's a great kid. Adult, I guess, but … you know what I mean. I love him. And when Palmer told me the truth recently, I resented that she wasn't honest. That she didn't think I was man enough to accept everything she is."

"Sometimes it's not quite that simple."

I nodded, staring down at my hands. "I still love her. I think I love her even more now, because I know what it's like to be without her. Seeing her with Danny … I know what kind of mother she'd be, and there's no one better."

"You hit it off with her brother right away, didn't you?" Dad said, grinning. "That didn't surprise me, because you once got your ass kicked as a kid defending another kid on the playground. He was in a wheelchair."

I nodded. "Yeah. I guess I admire people who have to work harder for things. I probably told you Danny and I hit it off instantly, but the truth is … the first meeting was …" I cringed and then laughed at the memory.

Dad gave me a quizzical look.

"Palmer wanted me to meet her mom and Danny," I said. "We'd been dating for a month, and things were going really well.

But she wanted to start small, so she asked me to pick her up for a date at her mom's house. I get there, and she introduces me to her brother, and he seems to like me okay, so I pull some peanut brittle I bought for him out of my coat and try to hand it to him. I'd stopped at the drug store on the way there, and it seemed like a good pick."

Dad was trying not to smile, but clearly was wondering where this story was headed.

"Next thing I know," I continued, "Palmer's mom Janelle is practically tackling me. She pretty much drop kicks the peanut brittle across the room. Apparently Danny has a peanut allergy, but I had no idea. So Danny bursts into tears and Janelle's about to pass out from panic. I apologized about fifteen times and Palmer dragged me out of there. I thought I was done for."

"That's an innocent mistake," Dad said.

"Yeah, but I was sure Janelle would think of me as 'that asshole who nearly killed my son' after that. But we were laughing about it the next time she saw me. She really is a great lady. And now … she's in bad shape, Dad."

I sighed deeply, letting the tears well.

"Sounds like Palmer needs you more than ever."

I nodded. "Yeah. Danny, too. I need to get my shit together."

The room started emptying and I looked at the clock. Never had I thought I'd be sorry to see visiting time ending. Dad stood, and I walked around the table to hug him.

"I love you," he said softly. "And I love your brother, too. Don't take this out on him."

I pulled away and met Dad's eyes. "He's clean. Has been for almost a year. I ride his ass constantly. We're business partners now."

Dad's eyes widened with surprise. "Troy? Good for you. How is he with the business end of things?"

"Well ... I handle all of that. But he's a hard worker. I'll take care of him, Dad."

He nodded and clapped me on the shoulder.

"Will you come back?" he asked.

"I'll be back next week."

He smiled, and I waved and headed through the door to the waiting area. I had a lot of information to sort through. I'd have to take the long way home.

Palmer

Porcelain tile colors and patterns ran through my head as I raised a forkful of chopped-up pasta to Danny's mouth. Georges and I had been brainstorming the backsplash for one of Derek and Adriane's many bathrooms when I left work this afternoon, and I was still running through our final list of options.

"Did you and Amanda go for a walk this afternoon?" I asked Danny.

"Manda."

I knew they'd gone for a walk – she'd told me when I got home, but I liked asking Danny about his day anyway.

"Did you see any squirrels?" I asked, suppressing a yawn. It was a little after 7 pm, which was late for us to be eating dinner. But I'd been busy mowing the grass and putting away laundry when I got home.

"Yeah," Danny said, grinning.

"Do you want more?" I scraped the bowl and gave him the last bite in it.

His lopsided nod made me smile. I wasn't a great cook, but Danny always enthusiastically ate whatever I made.

"Mom?" he asked, looking around the room.

"She's taking a bath, sweetie. I'll go check on her while this pasta cools down."

I added two big scoops to his bowl and set it down, grabbing a piece of garlic bread to eat on the way to the bathroom.

"Mom?" I called through the crack in the door. "You good?"

"No," she said weakly. My heart skipped a beat as I pushed the door open and walked in, averting my eyes from her, naked in the tub.

"What's wrong?"

"I can't get out," she said. Her helpless tone made me fly into action.

"I'll help you. No big deal."

"I'm flat on my back in here. The harder I tried to get out, the further I slid down."

I reached into a cabinet and grabbed a towel, unfolding it and draping it over her body.

"You're so cold," I said when my fingers brushed her shoulder.

"Yeah. I managed to pull the plug with my toe because the water was getting cold, but no water is much colder."

"Why didn't you call for me?"

"I did," she said. "Guess I'm not very loud anymore. I'm so tired and weak."

"Let's get you to bed," I said, reaching underneath her. "Can you wrap your arms around my neck?"

Her arms barely moved before dropping back to her sides. "I'm sorry. I used all my energy trying to get out of here."

"It's okay," I said, gingerly working my arms beneath her.

"Palmer, I don't think you can lift me. Don't hurt yourself."

I braced myself, preparing to show her I had this under control. But lifting with my legs was impossible when I was kneeling. I strained and couldn't even get her off the floor of the tub.

"Okay," I said, taking a deep breath. "Let's rethink this."

Even if I got her out of the tub without hurting one of us – which was unlikely – she needed to be carried to bed, and I couldn't do that.

"I think I need to call Jeremy," I said, referring to the next-door neighbor who I knew we could rely on in an emergency.

Mom cringed and closed her eyes. "But I'm naked. I don't want him seeing me like this."

I sighed, considering. Georges? No way. He wasn't much stronger than me. The only person who could help was the one I'd been avoiding since our recent fight.

"I'm calling Brady," I said, getting up. "And I'll be right in with a blanket for you."

I walked through the kitchen to dig my phone from my purse, and Danny looked at me, his brow furrowed with worry.

"Everything's okay," I said, touching my screen to dial Brady.

I went to the front door and stepped onto the front porch so Danny wouldn't hear the conversation.

"Palmer?" Brady said, sounding both surprised and concerned.

"I'm so sorry to be asking this," I started. "I know you're mad at me."

"What's wrong? Are you okay?"

"I need help. My mom … she's stuck in the bathtub. She's too weak to get herself out, and I can't get her out either."

"I'll be right there."

"Thank you." My voice broke with emotion and I swallowed, trying to gather myself.

"Hey, it'll be okay," Brady said softly. "I'm on my way, okay?"

"Okay."

I said goodbye to him and went inside, pulling a blanket from a closet in the living room. When I tucked it around Mom, she assured me she was okay and I went back to the kitchen to feed Danny.

He'd polished off the second serving of pasta and was halfway through some chocolate pudding when a knock sounded at the door.

"Hey," Brady said when I opened it. He still wore his navy Grant Brothers Builders t-shirt and jeans and I wondered if he'd still been working when I called.

"Hi. Thanks for coming. I hope I'm not taking you from something important."

He shook his head and stepped through the open door. "What's more important than this?"

I looked down at the floor. "She's ... come on, I'll take you to the bathroom."

"Does she have a robe or something I can cover her with?"

"I've got a blanket on her."

I led the way into the tiny bathroom and he smiled at my mom when he entered. The blue blanket couldn't hide the fact that her body was wasting and frail, but if Brady noticed, he didn't say so.

"Hi, Janelle."

"Brady. It's good to see you, even though I'm completely embarrassed."

He waved a hand and bent down to her. "Good to see you, too. And you're kinda helping me out here, 'cause nothing builds a man's ego like helping a damsel in distress."

I stood back, watching him bend and reach beneath her knees and shoulders. He stood and lifted her effortlessly.

"Where to, my lady?" he asked her, grinning.

"I never thought a handsome man would carry me to bed again," Mom said, smiling back. "My bedroom is out this door and to the right."

I followed him, ready to tuck her blanket back over her if it slipped, but Brady was so slow and gentle with her that nothing moved. He eased her down to her bed and looked at me.

"I can get her dressed," I said. "Thank you so much, Brady."

My mom thanked him, too, and he winked at her before walking out. I pushed the door closed and went to Mom's dresser to get her pajamas.

"He smells good," Mom murmured. "Kind of sweet."

"It's the smell of fresh cut wood. He always smells like that. I like it too."

I pulled the blanket away and she turned her head, embarrassed.

"Nothing I haven't seen before," I said, easing a nightshirt over her head. "And you've seen all my parts, too."

"Are you and Brady seeing each other again?"

There was hope in her tone, and I remembered her disappointment when I'd told her he and I were over.

"Kind of," I said, wanting to be honest but tactful. "We're not really going on dates, per se."

"Sleeping together?"

I was talking about my sex life with my mom while putting her underwear on for her. I'd never, ever imagined such a scenario.

"Well ... yeah," I said, feeling sheepish.

"There's nothing wrong with that, Palmer. It means things are still alive between you two."

I helped her settle onto her pillow and then sat down on the end of the bed.

"But things are different now. It's not the same."

Mom's eyes crinkled at the corners as she studied me. "Good. Things needed to be different. They weren't working before."

"But we fight," I said, playing with a loose thread on her bedspread. "And the sex is a lot more …" I struggled for words that were appropriate.

"Palmer, you just saw my hoo-ha. And I'm your mother. Just say it."

I smiled. "It's harder. Rougher. It feels a lot more raw than it used to."

"More passionate," she said. "There are a lot of feelings there for both of you. And you should be fighting. You can't get past the issues you split up over without fighting about them. But fighting and having rough sex is a hell of a lot better than avoiding each other and letting the hard feelings fester."

"I wish I wouldn't have let him go," I admitted.

"He's here, isn't he?"

"He's probably gone by now." I looked at the back of the closed door. Mom's yawn made me turn back to her.

"Well, that was my excitement for the night," she said. "Brady's a good man. I'm glad he's back in your life."

I kissed her forehead and tucked the covers over her shoulders. "Goodnight, Mom. Love you."

"Love you, too."

I left the room, pulling the door closed behind me. My tension started to drain away as I leaned against the door and exhaled. But the sound of Brady's voice put me back on high alert.

When I walked into the kitchen, he was there, raising a spoon to Danny's mouth. He was feeding him the rest of the chocolate pudding. Looking at the two of them made tears burn in my eyes.

"Thanks," I said, approaching and looking at the nearly empty bowl.

"No problem." Brady's green eyes were soft and warm, and I read the message he was sending me: I would've been doing this all along if you'd have let me.

"I need to give Danny his bath and get him to bed, but if you want to watch TV or something ... we could hang out when I'm done?" I said, eyeing him for a response.

"Yeah. But why don't I help with the bath, if Danny wants me to?"

Danny's face glowed with happiness as he reached for the wheels of his chair. I suppressed a sigh of relief. My back was sore from my effort to lift Mom out of the tub, and on a good day it took everything I had to help Danny from the wheelchair into the tub and back again.

Brady and I chatted about Derek and Adriane's house and played with Danny. It was funny how making bubble beards and drawing on the bathtub walls with Brady and my naked adult brother didn't feel weird. Preserving Danny's dignity mattered to Brady, whether or not Danny even realized what dignity was.

We dried and dressed him together, and Brady helped Danny into his bed.

"'Night, Danny," he said.

"Brady," Danny said, grinning at him.

"I have to go make a call," Brady said to me. "I'll meet you in the living room."

Nodding, I wondered briefly what he'd been doing when I called. Hopefully it had nothing to do with a woman.

Bathing Danny and tucking him in with Brady had filled me with a warm, comfortable feeling. This was so ... domestic. This was what parents did for their children. I'd imagined Brady and I doing this together one day, but never like this.

Though this was very different than the dreams I'd once had, it was enough in this moment. Things were hard and I was stressed, but I wasn't alone.

I turned on a baseball game and read Danny a story, and his eyelids were drooping when I kissed him on the forehead. Brady was sitting on the couch when I pulled Danny's door closed and walked into the living room.

"I really appreciate you coming over so quickly to help me," I said.

"I'm glad you called me."

"Were you busy?"

He shook his head, putting his arm around the back of the couch. Too bad I'd sat down too far away for his arm to be around me.

"I was entering time sheets for the guys working here. My secretary usually does it, but she's in Colorado, so I have to do it for the job here."

I arched my brows and smiled. "You have a secretary? For some reason that makes me feel really proud of you."

He shrugged. "Yeah, Kathy's great. I couldn't get by without her."

There was a moment of awkward silence before he spoke again.

"I mean, she's happily married and her first grandchild was just born, so I don't mean for it to sound like … you know."

His earnest expression made me move a seat closer to him. I tried for a pouty, seductive look, hoping he'd get the hint.

"I'd offer you a drink, but we don't have anything good," I said, gathering my hair over one shoulder. My bare neck always seemed to turn Brady on for some reason.

A small smile played on his lips as he took one of my hands and laced his fingers into mine.

"I know what you need right now," he said.

"Oh, really?" A warm buzz of arousal spread through me as I looked into his bright green eyes.

"C'mon." He patted his lap.

"Oh, so it's like that?" I asked playfully, climbing to my knees to straddle him.

He surprised me by pulling me into his lap and wrapping his big arms around me. I definitely wasn't straddling him. He was cradling me, which didn't feel at all sexy.

"What's this?" I asked, confused.

"No sex. I just want to be with you, Palmer. I want you to let go. You keep such a brave face on for your mom and Danny, but you don't have to with me. Real intimacy isn't about sex – it's about sharing your feelings."

"How are you feeling?" I asked, tilting my head back so I could look at his face.

He lifted one corner of his mouth in a smile. "I've got mixed emotions right now," he said softly. "I'm happy you called me when you needed something. Grateful you trust me enough to let me help during such a difficult time. Hurting over seeing your mom like she is. Helpless from seeing you upset."

I wanted to respond, but I couldn't speak past the giant lump in my throat. This was the man I'd assumed would be bothered by my burdens, and instead he actually wanted to help me bear them.

"I'm so glad you're here right now," I said, my voice thick. "So grateful that even though we fought, you care enough to come running when I need you. I'm sad you aren't mine anymore. And I'm so damn scared about what's going to happen to my mom. Seeing her in that bathtub tonight reminded me that she's getting worse fast. I'm not ready for this, Brady. I can cope as long as she's still here, but I'm not ready to lose her."

I released the sob I'd been holding in, burying my face in his chest and crying like I'd only ever done alone. I held nothing back, letting all the anguish pour out of me while he held on and rocked me gently.

Eventually, I wore down to just sniffling, lulled by the comfort of Brady's solid, warm body cradling me against him. I jumped at the sound of a knock on the door.

"Who in the hell could that be?" I mumbled. "I don't want to answer the door like this."

"I've got it." Brady rose, picking me up and setting me back on the couch. He opened the door and reached for something. I couldn't see who was on the doorstep from my spot on the couch, but I guessed when I got a whiff of cheese and pepperoni.

He turned and closed the door, balancing several items on top of a cardboard box.

"Uh ... pizza delivery?" I asked, puzzled.

"Better," he said with a grin. "My brother. We've got pizza, chocolate cake and wine."

"God that sounds good." I got up from couch and headed for the kitchen. "I can't get drunk, but I can have a glass of wine. And some cake. That was so sweet of Troy."

Brady grunted and rolled his eyes. "I called and told him to bring it."

"Well, it was still sweet."

I poured wine into two glass tumblers and handed him one. He dove into the pizza and I ate several forkfuls of chocolate cake.

"Can I stay with you tonight?" he asked, looking at me from across Mom's tiny kitchen island. There was a note of pleading in his eyes.

I didn't even want to think about him leaving tonight. "Yes. I only have a twin bed downstairs, though."

"That's fine with me." He drained his glass of wine and picked up the pizza box. "Want to head down? You look really tired."

I nodded and grabbed the wine bottle. As soon as I got to the bottom of the stairs, I turned on the receivers for the baby monitors I kept in Mom and Danny's bedroom so I could hear them if they needed something during the night.

When I turned back to Brady, he was sitting on the worn out brown sofa my Mom had owned since before I was born, untying his work boots and taking them off.

"Hey," I said softly. "Not that I want to bring it back up, because I don't, but ... the fight we had. I'm sorry. Not just because you're here tonight. I was sorry the moment you left my house. I said some spiteful things."

He sighed and rested his elbows on his knees. "I'm sorry, too. I lost my temper, which I never wanted to do again with you. Believe it or not, I'm level-headed most of the time. But you make me into a ..." He gestured his hands with frustration. "... a giant puddle of feelings. I think maybe it's the nature of us together. The highs are higher, and the lows are lower."

"Wanna hug it out in bed?" I asked, cocking my brows at him.

"We're not having sex tonight. I'll give you a massage and then we're going to bed."

"I've never known you to not want sex." I tried to keep my tone casual, but the hurt made its way in.

"I do want it, Palmer. But you had an upsetting night, and I just want to be here with you. We're more than just fuck buddies, right?"

I suppressed a smile. He had me there. "Right."

"Okay, then." He stood and pulled his t-shirt off over his head. "Shirt off. Lay down on your stomach."

I complied, moaning when he started working his magic on my shoulders. His hands were big and strong, capable of kneading away all my tension with just the right amount of pressure.

Surprisingly, I was relieved. I'd wanted sex because it would take my mind away from the anxiety I felt over my mom after seeing her so helpless tonight. But wine, chocolate cake and a massage had eased my worries. I knew it wasn't really any of those things, though. It was Brady, not just telling me, but showing me that there was still more left of us than just hot sex.

Chapter 13

Brady

I scrubbed a hand down my face and exhaled deeply, reading over the time sheets and update Kathy had sent me for the commercial job in Denver.

"What the fuck is all this overtime about?" I said to the empty room.

Kathy answered from speaker of the phone on my desk. "I told Adam to cut overtime two weeks ago, and then I get these time sheets. This job is over budget and behind schedule."

"Yeah, no shit," I muttered. "Adam knows you get to decide on overtime when I'm not there. What's his explanation?"

"He just said it had to be done. Then he told me to stick to paperwork and let him handle the Stanton job."

I glared at the phone. "He said that to you?"

"Oh, I set him straight, don't worry." Kathy's no-nonsense tone filled the trailer that was my on-site office at the Chicago work site. "I told him he'd find my foot so far up his ass he'd be able to taste the leather of my heels if he sassed me again."

"Good. I'm gonna say something to him anyway, though." I leaned back in my chair and stared at the numbers on the computer screen. It was impossible to be in two places at once, but that was what I needed to do.

"What do you want me to do about the overtime?" Kathy asked.

"Pay it." I minimized the time sheets on my screen so I wouldn't have to stare at the diminishing profit for the job any longer. "I'll be there tomorrow night so I can get this job back in line."

"How's that job coming along?"

"It's good," I said. "Ahead of schedule."

"Probably because you're the foreman."

I grunted my agreement. "Can you run some numbers on bonusing the Stanton crew if the job comes in on the schedule and budget I give them? Make it worth their while."

"I'll send you something this afternoon."

"You're the best, Kathy. See you Thursday morning."

"Safe travels, boss."

I already knew I'd stew the entire trip and then rip Adam a new asshole when I got to Denver. Good help was hard to find, but employees who cared about keeping my jobs on track as much as I did? Well, that was fucking impossible. No one kept an eye on every last detail the way I did.

But damn, was this lousy timing. Palmer was finally starting to lean on me for more than just sex. I wanted to show her I meant it when I said I'd be there for her. And how the hell could I be there for her from Denver?

I had no choice but to go. As much as I hated it, I had to go reign in the out of control Stanton job. I'd worked too hard building this company to drain my reserves on this one job.

I'd liked being so crazy busy with my job that I had no time for a personal life. Up until now.

Palmer

Mom reached out for a cup on the counter, but her hand seemed stuck in space next to it. She let her hand drop to the counter for a few seconds before trying again.

"Here," I said, hurrying over to pick it up for her.

"What?" She looked at me blankly.

"The cup. You were trying to get it."

"I don't want that."

My phone vibrated in my pocket, and I silenced it. Probably just Georges calling about the meeting we were having with Adriane tomorrow to go over design progress on her house.

Mom squinted at me, as though she'd just realized I was standing there.

"Palmer," she said softly. "I'm sorry for missing your homecoming game."

My heart twisted in my chest. I hadn't thought about that in forever. I'd been crowned Homecoming Princess my junior year of high school, and the parents of the court had all come to the homecoming football game to be introduced at halftime. I'd been alone and mortified when I had to walk across that field by myself when everyone else had at least one parent with them.

"That was forever ago, Mom. Let's get you into bed." I rubbed her back in soothing circles. "I'll settle you in and get you some tea."

When I wrapped an arm around her shoulders, the bones beneath my hand reminded me why I couldn't sleep these days. Like her clarity, her strength seemed to fade by the day.

I wished Amanda was still here. She'd left for her second shift job forty-five minutes ago. Just having her stay for a few minutes when I got home from work every afternoon had shown me what it was like to have an extra set of hands when I needed help.

"Danny, stay at the table, okay?" I turned and met his gaze as I was leaving the room with Mom. There was a pot of boiling water on the stove, and though I knew it was unlikely he'd approach it, I didn't like leaving him alone in the room right now.

He nodded, his brow pinched with worry. Even though he knew Mom was sick, to him that meant throwing up or a runny nose. He couldn't seem to process what was happening to her, and I didn't know how to help.

Mom shuffled beside me, and slowly we made it to her darkened bedroom. I led her to the bed and helped her lay down.

"Okay?" I asked, pulling the covers up to her chest. She nodded, her eyes half closed already.

I closed the door halfway and went back to the kitchen to finish dinner. Danny was playing with a big deck of colored cards Amanda was using to teach him.

"You want a regular grilled cheese or an extra cheesy one?" I asked. "I'm making grilled cheese and ravioli."

"Cheese!" Danny answered.

"Extra cheesy, then." I opened the refrigerator and scanned the contents. "I need to get groceries, don't I?"

I pulled out the butter and cheese, my thoughts wandering to Brady as I made sandwiches. I missed him. Since leaving for Denver last week, he'd called me every day. I'd started expecting his nightly call around 9 pm– looking forward to it, even. But what would happen when this job was over and he was back in Denver permanently?

The sandwiches browned on the griddle while I considered relocating to be with Brady. Did he even want that? Even if he did, it would be tough. I didn't have much money, and Danny had grown attached to Amanda. She'd taken him to the facility she worked at a few times and I was considering taking her advice and enrolling him in a program there.

But now that he was back in my life, I didn't know if I could let him go again. No other man would ever compare to Brady. He was my strong, solid perfection, even with his tendency to brood.

"Red!" Danny cried, holding up a card.

"Yes! Red," I said, smiling. "Good job."

I scooped the sandwiches from the griddle and dished ravioli onto plates. Danny wanted me to quiz him on colors while the food cooled down, so I held up the cards one at a time and clapped when he got them right.

By the time I'd fed him, eaten myself and cleaned up the kitchen, it was bath time. I helped Danny into his chair, wheeling him to Mom's room, where I stopped outside the doorway.

"Just gonna check on Mom," I said to him.

She was sitting up in bed, but I couldn't see much besides the outline of her. I came closer and made out her vacant stare.

"Mom?"

"Wh-what?"

She turned to me and an ominous sensation crept up my spine. I sat down on the bed and smoothed a hand over her hair.

"Are you okay?" I asked.

"What?"

"Mom, what do you need? Are you having pain?"

My heart was beating wildly as she stared back, her eyes void of emotion.

"What?"

I swallowed past the lump in my throat.

"Say something else for me, Mom. Can you say anything else?"

"What?"

I got up and ran for my phone on the kitchen counter.

"Almer?" Danny called behind me.

I dialed Amanda, who answered on the second ring.

"Palmer? Everything okay?"

"No. Something's wrong with my mom. She's only saying one word and I feel like she doesn't even recognize me. Should I call hospice?"

"You should call an ambulance."

My tears spilled over. "Okay. Thanks."

"Do you need me to leave work and come watch Danny?" she asked. "I can probably get out of here."

"No, I'll – I have a neighbor who can come. And I'll call my aunt and uncle. But thanks."

"Let me know what's going on, okay?"

I agreed and hung up, dialing 911 on the way back to Mom's bedroom. As I gave them her address and information, I wiped my cheeks and sat down on the bed, rubbing her arm reassuringly.

She was agitated now, shifting and looking around the room in confusion.

"Okay, it's okay, Mom," I said. She slid over to the edge of the bed and tried to get out, but I held her in place. "Stay in bed for now. Help's on the way. It's okay."

She tried to pull away, but she was too weak. I looked into her eyes, hoping to reassure her, but her eyes were wide with terror. Tears pooled, hanging in the balance, and her body shook in my arms.

Please, I prayed silently. Please don't let this be the end. *Not with Danny right outside the door and her so scared. I know it's close, but please don't let this be it.*

I had to hold on and stay strong until help arrived. I was wondering how long it would be when I remembered that I'd locked the door when Amanda left. I couldn't leave Mom like this to answer the door. Not when she was trying to get out of bed and could fall.

I dialed 911 again, explaining who I was to the dispatcher.

"Tell them to force the door," I said. "Break it down if they have to. I can't get there to open it."

Mom was wild-eyed now, her gaze wandering around the room like she was looking for an escape. I held her close, trying to reassure her. It was only a couple of minutes until I heard the front door being forced open, but they were the longest minutes of my life.

A young woman dressed in a paramedic uniform flipped on the lights and walked into the room, a muscular middle-aged man right behind her.

"She has metastatic lung cancer that's in her brain now, too," I said. "Something's not right."

"No!" Mom cried, wiggling free of my grasp and glaring at me.

"Ma'am, we're here to help," the female paramedic said, kneeling beside the bed. "Can you tell me your name?"

Mom gave her the same blank stare she'd given me.

"What's your name?" the paramedic asked again.

"What?"

Another paramedic was comforting Danny in the hallway. I closed my eyes, wishing for my mom. Though she was in my arms right now, she really wasn't here. And I was terrified the part of her that knew me was gone forever.

"We'll take her to the hospital," the paramedic said to me. "You're her daughter?"

"Yes. Can I come, too?"

"Sure."

I took a deep breath, grateful when I had to move aside so they could take Mom's blood pressure and help her onto the gurney they'd rolled into the room.

"I have to go ask my neighbor to stay with my brother," I said, rushing from the room.

As soon as I opened the door and stepped into the muggy summer air, I gave in to my overwhelming urge to cry. This was my chance. I'd have to be strong and comfort Danny as soon as I got back in. I'd have to hold it together after that to be with Mom at the hospital.

This was my chance. And I took it, letting the tension and worry and sadness take over until I was sobbing. There was nothing I could do. The fatigue I often fought from taking care of Mom and Danny while working – that I could handle indefinitely. But this? Sitting by while my mom was scared and hurting? It was worse than knowing she was dying.

Brady

I flipped the switch on my office coffeemaker and it gurgled to life. It was only a little past 8 pm, but my ass was dragging. Too many early mornings and late nights on site and in this damned office since I'd gotten home to Colorado. And when I did finally leave here and crawl into bed at my apartment, I couldn't sleep much. I always had too much on my mind. Sometimes work. Sometimes my dad. But usually Palmer.

One more hour 'til I called her. I always waited until Danny was in bed so she could relax and get comfortable while we talked. It was so easy to picture her curled up on the couch or in her bed, wine glass in hand that she sipped from during our conversation.

It was my own damned fault we'd been apart for the past year. I knew that now, and I felt like shit about it. When Palmer needed me most, I'd been building my business in another state and fucking other women. My stupid pride had let her one comment about not needing me change everything.

I scrubbed a hand down my face as I watched the coffeepot fill up. Another couple of late nights here, and hopefully I'd be able to go back to Chicago for a few days.

After I poured some coffee, I went to the office refrigerator and found the sandwich Kathy had left me. I was on my way back to my desk to eat when my phone buzzed from my pocket.

Palmer. I smiled over not having to wait an hour to hear her voice.

"Hey, how are you?" I answered.

There was a pause before she broke into a sob. "Awful."

Fucking hell. It had to be her mom. I tossed the sandwich on a counter and pressed my hand to my forehead. Hearing her cry made my chest tighten uncomfortably.

"The doctor thinks she had a seizure." Palmer sighed, her voice still shaky. "She didn't recognize me and I had to call an ambulance."

I closed my eyes, wishing like hell I was with her right now. "I'm so sorry. Are you okay?"

"Yeah. She started coming out of it when we got here. But the doctor said it could happen again. It's the tumors in her brain."

"What about Danny? You need me to come home and help with him?"

"My aunt and uncle are on the way. Mom's brother and his wife."

I felt a small measure of relief that she had family coming. The thought of Palmer, alone at the hospital, was crushing.

"I'll come back early," I said.

"You don't have to do that. You'll be here in a few days, right?"

"Yeah, but … I feel like I should be there now."

"Just hearing your voice makes me feel better, Brady. And knowing you'll be here."

She was going for confidence with her tone, but I heard vulnerability.

"Palmer, I—"

"Hey, the doctor is going into Mom's room, I have to go. I'll call you tomorrow, okay?"

"Yeah."

I wanted to tell her I loved her, but something held the words in my mouth.

"Bye, Brady."

"Bye."

I hung up, leaning both palms on the counter and considering. No way could I think about paperwork now. There was only one person who could help. Good thing he owed me a favor.

Palmer

The crack of light in the room got larger as a nurse pushed the door open. I lifted my face from Mom's bed, my neck protesting with an ache since I'd dozed off while leaning over the side of my chair.

"Just checking her vitals," the nurse whispered, rolling a small cart in front of her. I glanced at Mom, who was still sleeping.

"Is there coffee out there?" I asked softly. The nurse nodded and directed me to a drink station around the corner. I headed that way, my head heavy and foggy.

That had been the first time I'd gone to sleep all night. The nurse came in once every hour to check on Mom, and I watched, bleary-eyed and relieved when her blood pressure and pulse were normal.

The coffee wasn't half bad, considering it was almost three in the morning. But coffee was probably a staple around here. I was halfway through my Styrofoam cup when the elevator doors near the drink station opened and a dark figure stepped out.

Brady. Disbelief flooded me, followed immediately by a sense of gratitude that made my knees unsteady.

"You're here," I said, setting my cup down on the counter. "How?"

He covered the last few steps between us and took me in his arms, holding me tight for a few seconds before speaking.

"I had to come. I needed to be here. I've got a friend with a plane who flew me in."

I pulled away to meet his warm green eyes. "Your friends are cooler than mine."

He smiled and leaned his forehead down to touch mine. "He's a client. I built his house."

"I'm so glad you're here." I reached up and ran a hand through his thick, dark hair. "I know I said you didn't have to come, but—"

"Yeah, I figured it must've been reverse psychology, because last time you said that I listened and everything went to shit."

I wanted to admonish him, but I couldn't help laughing against his chest. God, it felt good to release some of my bottled tension.

"I wasn't playing games," I said. "I meant it, but … I'm really glad you didn't listen."

"You're just used to doing everything on your own. You don't have to do that, you know."

My body deflated as I sighed. "It's hard to ask for help. Everything about this is hard."

He pulled me against his chest again, speaking softly in my ear. "You want to talk, or try to sleep?"

I yawned, despite the cup of coffee. "I'm just drained. Worn out, but I don't know if I can sleep."

"You want me in the room with you?" Brady asked. "'Cause I can crash on the couch in the lounge."

"Of course I want you in there. There's only a recliner and a tiny chair in there, though."

We turned to walk toward Mom's room, his arm draped over my shoulders.

"Hey," he said softly. "I had a hell of a time talking my way past security to get in here. If anyone asks, we're married, okay?"

It sounded more than okay. I only wished it was true. As I nodded and sank against Brady, I realized I could've had this for the past year. Could've had him. Instead, I'd told him to go to Colorado and start over. His life was there now, and he'd be returning to it eventually.

But for now, he was here. I was Mom's source of comfort, and it felt so good to know Brady was here to be mine.

Chapter 14

Brady

Janelle couldn't weigh more than eighty pounds. She was skin and bones – too fragile to even spend energy smiling and making small talk like she always had. When I lifted her from the wheelchair into Palmer's car, her gratitude made her eyes shine, but she was silent.

My whole body was tight with the tension of being as gentle as I could. I lowered her to the seat gingerly, worried about hurting her. Palmer looked at me from the other side of the back seat, where she was leaning though the door of her sedan.

"Okay, Mom?" she said. "Ready to go home?"

"I'll drive," I said. "You can sit back here with her."

Palmer nodded and slid in, handing me the keys. When I got into the driver's seat, my knees were crushed against the steering wheel. Fucking small cars. I wished I had my truck to drive them home in, but I'd left it in Colorado.

I moved the seat back, which helped a little, and we drove home in relative silence. When I looked in the rearview mirror, Janelle's head was resting on Palmer's shoulder and Palmer was smoothing Janelle's short, spiky hair.

My breath caught for a second. There was so much love in that woman. No matter the toll it took on her, she was strong and nurturing for her mom and brother. She never let go in front of them.

Her eyes caught mine in the mirror and the corners of her lips turned up just a touch. I was so glad I'd followed my instinct about coming here. Work could wait. I needed to be with Palmer right now.

When we got to Janelle's tiny ranch house, there was a note on the counter from the home health aide Palmer had hired. She'd taken Danny to the place she worked for the day.

I carried Janelle from the car into her bedroom, where Palmer tucked her in and brought in a glass of water for the night stand. Janelle's eyes slid closed immediately, and Palmer's face fell with exhaustion.

"I need to rest, too," she said, sliding her shoes off. She approached and wrapped her arms around my neck. I held her against me, wishing I could do more to alleviate her worry and fatigue.

"You're amazing," I whispered in her ear.

"So are you. Can you come over for dinner tonight? Will you still be in town?"

"Yep. I'll be here."

She pressed the side of her face to my chest, relaxing into me. "It'll be something really gourmet like spaghetti," she murmured.

"I'll bring dinner. Sleep, and I'll see you tonight, okay?"

She nodded and moved away, entwining her fingers with mine before our hands fell apart and she crawled into bed beside her mom. She'd hardly slept at the hospital and I knew she'd be out in minutes.

I went outside and texted Troy to come pick me up. I dialed Kathy while I waited.

"Morning," she said brightly. "You planning on showing up today?"

"Ah ... I'm actually in Chicago."

"Chicago! Did you drive all night? Is everything okay?"

I sighed deeply. "It's ... pretty okay, I guess. I had to get back to be with someone who has a sick family member."

"Oh. I'm sorry, Brady. Who do you want to be foreman on Stanton until you get back?"

I shook my head. There were no good choices. Kathy filled the silence with a sympathetic murmur.

"You could send Hunter here," she suggested. "He's got your back."

"Yeah, but he's so fuckin' passive. He's afraid of pissing the guys off."

Another murmur, this one in agreement. "Adam?" Kathy offered.

"Hell no. I'm on the verge of firing him."

"I know this is rotten timing, but this job has to have a strong leader right now. We're just barely back on budget."

"I know that," I said, my irritation coming through in my tone.

"Don't shoot the messenger," Kathy said.

"I'm not. It's not you. I'm just in a bad spot right now."

Troy cruised to a stop in Palmer's driveway, driving the beat-up red pickup he'd fixed up with Dad when he was in high school.

"For now, you're the foreman," I said to Kathy.

"Me?" she shrieked. "Oh, hell no."

"It's temporary. You can do it from the office, you don't have to be on site."

"Brady ..." she protested.

"Please, Kathy. Just for today and tomorrow keep shit from exploding, alright?"

"Okay. But I will send home anyone who gives me an ounce of shit."

I smiled. "Please do. I owe you, Kathy."

"You're damn straight."

We said our goodbyes and I climbed into Troy's truck. He scowled at me, specks of drywall dust making his eyebrows more white than black.

"You sheet-rockin' today?" I asked.

"What the hell are you doing here? You're supposed to be in Denver. And whose house is this?"

"Relax, *Mom*. It's Palmer's mom's place. I came back last night 'cause she's in really bad shape."

"Last night? I talked to you at the office at six. Did you drive all night?"

"I flew."

His eyes bulged. "Flew?"

"Joel flew me."

"Joel? As in Joel Davenport?"

I nodded. Troy shook his head as he glanced over his shoulder to back out of the driveway.

"You two are some damn friendly exes," he said.

"What's it to you?"

"Nothing." He shrugged. "Where am I taking you?"

"Back to our apartment. I haven't slept."

Troy nodded, and we drove in silence for a minute.

"You been to visit Dad?" I asked.

"Nope."

"Why not?"

He stared ahead at the road, his expression giving nothing away.

"What's it to you?" he finally asked, stealing my line.

"Why not?" I repeated, more firmly this time.

"I don't feel like seeing him. After what he did, can you blame me?"

"Yeah, kinda," I said. "Considering *why* he did it."

Troy's jaw tensed. "What the fuck is that supposed to mean?"

"What's it mean to you?" I asked.

"I don't know why he did it, and I don't fucking care, Brady. I'm over it."

I shook my head, disgusted. "I know you're lying on one count, and I sure as shit hope you're lying on the other, too. You know why, Troy. And you'd better care. I'll beat you ass into caring if you don't."

"Yeah, fine, Brady," he said, his voice shaking and venomous at the same time. "Dad's probably in jail because of me. I'm the prodigal son, does that make you feel even more superior?"

I furrowed my brow. "I don't even know what the fuck that means. The fact that you can do so many drugs and stay so smart kind of blows my mind. And I've never felt superior."

"Bullshit." He scoffed and gave me a dirty look. "You've always been the oldest and the best."

"Is this where you blame me for your drug problem?" I rolled my eyes. "Man up and take some responsibility for once, Troy."

"I've been clean for almost a year."

"Yeah, and that's great. But how the hell do you leave Dad rotting in prison when he's there because he was helping you?"

Troy shook his head. "I don't know. Out of sight, out of mind I guess."

He pulled up in front of our apartment and threw the truck into park.

"Are you fuckin' kidding me?" I demanded, my voice rising. "You don't feel the least bit bad about it?"

"I feel like shit about it!" he roared, turning to me. "Why the fuck do you think I got clean? It was so he didn't go there for nothing."

"He wants to see you." I forced myself to calm down, though stress and sleeplessness had me on the edge.

"I can't." Troy turned away. "I'm too ... I don't know. He and Mom lost everything because of me. I can't face him."

My heart cracked for my kid brother, who had more going for him than he'd ever realized.

"You're gonna face him," I said. "You have to. He wants to see you. You're going there this afternoon."

"Brady, I can't. Not after all this time."

"He's our dad. Go. Or don't go, it's up to you. But you're leaving for Denver in the morning, so I think you should go."

He gave me a puzzled look. "Me? Am I going to pick up your truck?"

"No. You're going to take over as foreman on the Stanton job."

His mouth fell open as he stared at me. "What? Adam's the foreman."

"Actually, Kathy's acting foreman 'til you get there. And when you do, you'll be taking over all aspects of the job."

"The onsite stuff, you mean?"

I shook my head. "No. Everything. Prepare to work some long hours. That job is over budget and behind schedule. You know that. Fix it."

"That's way over my head, Brady. You should send Hunter."

"We're Grant Brothers Builders. Partners. And I've been managing too much workload from the beginning."

"Hogging, you mean," Troy said, arching his brows.

"Hogging? Really? Like we're kids or something?"

He shrugged. "It's the truth. You hog all the important work and leave me on the sheet-rock crew."

"Not anymore, baby brother."

"It's a big job, man," he said doubtfully. "Maybe you should start me on something smaller."

"You're ready. I trust you with it."

His look of alarm was obnoxious. "You got your fingers crossed behind your back or something?"

"Look, douchebag. Palmer's mom is dying. I need to be here with her, and that doesn't mean in my fucking office 'til ten every night managing the Denver work. Take over. Call me if you have questions, but lean on Kathy as much as you can. She knows her shit and she knows our business."

He let out a breath, nodding slowly. "Alright. I've got it. And I'm sorry about Palmer's mom."

"Thanks." I opened the truck door and stepped out, leaning in to say one last thing before closing the door. "Go see Dad, Troy. You'll be glad you did. The only person you need forgiveness from is you."

Palmer

My heart pounded with worry and I broke into a jog in Mom's driveway, rushing the rest of the way into her house. I'd had to work late finishing the nursery I designed, and I'd been thinking about Mom much of that time.

She was sleeping a lot now, but I still hated to be away from her. Every waking minute I feared she'd die, and I wouldn't be there. Even when I was at her house and I left her side for a moment, I was thinking about hurrying so I could get back to her.

When I walked in the front door, I was surprised to see Brady sitting on the couch with Danny, the empty wheelchair next to them.

"Hi," I said, setting my purse on a table. "I didn't see your truck."

"It's still in Denver. One of the guys dropped me off."

Danny wore his favorite threadbare Cubs t-shirt and had a pillow propped behind his back. His stare was fixated on the TV, so I knew it must be game time.

"Amanda's in with your mom," Brady said.

I walked over to them – just two guys hanging out watching the game. But that was something rare and special in our house. I leaned down to kiss Brady on the cheek and he slid a hand behind my neck, kissing me softly on the mouth.

"Missed you today," he murmured against my lips.

"Me too." I ran a hand over his cheek, the thought of a life that didn't include seeing him every day making my heart ache.

I kissed Danny's cheek next, and he looked away, leaning around me so he could see the TV screen. This bit of normalcy was exactly what I needed right now.

A single baseball card rested on the arm of the couch next to Danny.

"What's that?" I asked.

Brady broke out in a grin. "I brought him a pack of baseball cards, but he only wanted the one who's a Cub. Had to throw the others away."

I smiled back, standing to go into Mom's room just as Amanda walked out, leaving the door cracked open.

"I thought that was you," she said, approaching. "How was your day?"

"Okay. How is she?"

"Resting comfortably. Hospice came early this afternoon, so I think she'll sleep for a while."

I nodded, relaxing a little. "Do you want a glass of wine?"

Amanda followed me into the kitchen. "I can't before work, but thanks anyway."

I poured myself a glass, leaning against the kitchen counter as I sipped it. Even with the hint of bitterness, it went down easy. I didn't love wine, but was finding that half a glass helped relax me when I was wound tight over Mom these days.

"I think I'll tell my aunt and uncle not to come Friday night," I said, thinking out loud. "I can't leave her for a night."

Amanda's expression was sympathetic. "I think you need a night away more than ever. She won't go Friday night, I guarantee it."

"How can you know that?"

"There are signs when the end is days away, and she isn't there yet. Let your aunt and uncle come. Lean on hospice, and your boyfriend, and me. You know I'm here anytime, day or night, right?"

I smiled. "You've become like a member of the family. I hope you'll stay to help with Danny, ever after …"

She nodded. "I just became eligible to switch to day shift at work. I'm thinking about it, but it'd help with the decision if you'd enroll Danny in the day program. Then I could still be around him every day. I'm not suggesting it just because of me. He does so well there, Palmer. He really likes it. He's made friends."

I didn't bother holding back the tears that slid from the corners of my eyes. "I can't tell you how good that makes me feel. You've really opened my eyes about how much my brother can do. Things I never realized."

"Some of his friends live in a group home at the facility. It's a house, but they have care around the clock."

I nodded, feeling guilty because of Mom's aversion to Danny living anywhere but home.

"It's nothing you need to think about now," Amanda said. "But you should think about the day program."

She walked over and hugged me. "I have to go to work. Take care, okay? And sleep tonight. She's okay for now, I promise."

"Thanks."

She said goodbye to Danny and Brady and left as Brady was walking into the kitchen.

"Want me to go pick up some dinner?" he asked.

"I can throw something together. You don't need to bring us dinner every night."

"Palmer." He wrapped his arms around my waist from behind. "You don't need to be cooking right now."

"I'd definitely rather be sitting with her," I admitted.

"Go. I've got Danny tonight. I'll take him with me to get dinner. Okay if I use your car?"

"Of course."

I headed for Mom's bedroom, giving him a grateful glance. Tonight I could focus just on Mom. It was a luxury.

Her peaceful expression as she slept was comforting to me. She wasn't able to talk to me, but she was still here and she wasn't in pain. That was enough.

I sat down next to the bed and took her hand. Instead of focusing on its frailty, I thought about how warm it was. These hands had cradled me and Danny; fed us and bandaged our scrapes growing up. They had cooked us countless meals and folded our clean clothes into neat piles to be worn again.

My mom's hands had worked harder than most. Helping a man clean himself, feeding him and moving him from his chair to his bed – that kind of work wasn't something most people ever did year in and year out.

"Am I as good as you, Mom?" I whispered into the quiet dusk of the room. "Can I take care of Danny as well as you always have?"

She couldn't answer, but I felt a response inside myself. I wasn't doing it alone. I had help, and together, we cared for Danny like Mom did. It wasn't the same, but hopefully, it would be enough.

I talked to her. Once I started, the words poured out. I told her about the time I snuck out to go on a date when I was sixteen and felt guilty the entire time. I told her how much I resented my father for abandoning his family and leaving her to carry such a heavy load. But mostly, I told her about Brady. How scared I was of him leaving and how sorry I was for not being honest with him.

The faint rays of the sun that crept in the sides of the dark curtains faded, and I was getting up to leave when she stirred.

"Hmm?" she said, dazed.

"Hey," I whispered, squeezing her hand.

"Palmer."

"I'm here, Mom."

"Can I have some water?"

"Of course. I think it's time for your medicine, so I'll bring it in."

She sighed, sounding defeated. "I'm so tired. You better hurry or I'll be asleep again."

I went into the kitchen and noticed the living room was empty when I glanced over. When I got back to the bedroom, Mom barely lifted her head from the pillow so I could slide the pill in and help her take a sip of water. As soon as she swallowed, she dropped her head back down.

After I took the glass back to the kitchen, I stood by the sink thinking. Nothing anyone said could have prepared me for this. Words like "sad" and "difficult" didn't do it justice.

The sound of footsteps made me turn. Brady gave me a half smile.

"Danny's in bed," he said, a note of pride in his tone.

"Your shirt's all wet." I furrowed my brow in confusion.

"Bath time."

"You didn't have to do that."

He approached, squeezing my shoulders. "I don't mind."

"You've done so much for me. I really appreciate it."

His hands pressed into my shoulders slowly, working away the stress.

"That feels so good," I said softly.

"Shh," he whispered. "Just enjoy it or you're gonna make me hard."

I smiled and looked up to meet his dark green gaze.

"Mom's asleep. Can we go downstairs? I have another favor to ask."

"I'm liking the sound of this."

He took my hand and led me down the stairs to the tiny cave that was my bedroom here.

"Will you still be here Friday night?" I asked.

"I'm here indefinitely. I sent Troy to Denver."

The wave of relief that washed over me was almost palpable. I'd been wondering all day if he was leaving soon.

"I'm glad to hear that," I said. "Can you stay at my place Friday night? My house, not this one."

"Sure."

I sat down on the end of the bed, looking at the worn carpet to avoid his gaze.

"I want you to tie me up," I said. "I mean, tie me to my bed. Arms and legs. So I can't move."

His eyes narrowed into an expression of hunger that made me want to do it right now. But we had to wait. I didn't want anything else on my mind when we did this.

"And then what?" he asked in a low tone.

"Anything. Everything. As long as it's intense. I don't want you to hold back. Make it hurt. Make it so I can't feel anything else."

His lips parted a little, probably in shock. This was out of character for me, the woman who'd blushed the entire night he made love to me for the first time.

"I mean, if you want to," I said in a rush, my cheeks warming. "If that turns you on. I trust you, so it turns me on. But if you think it's weird—"

"No," he cut in, and I looked up at him. "I mean, yes. It turns me on. Look at me."

He gestured at his crotch, where his bulge strained against the fabric of his jeans. "I just … don't want to take things too far."

"How far have you taken it with other women?" I asked, bracing myself for his answer.

His eyed widened.

"You don't have to tell me." Now my face was flaming, and I regretted bringing this up.

"Palmer," he said softly, sitting down next to me on the bed. "Relax, baby. There's nothing you can't ask me. I've had rough sex before but I've never tied anyone up."

"Now I feel like a freak for asking."

Brady laughed, his low tone making me aware of how close he was right now. "You're not a freak. I'd love to do this with you."

"Really?"

"Absolutely. Are you kidding? You just have to promise you'll tell me if it's too much."

I hugged my arms to myself protectively. "Will you tell me something dirty you fantasize about so I don't feel quite so deviant?"

He was about to answer when I squeezed my eyes closed. "Sorry. I need to turn on the monitors so I can hear Mom and Danny. Sorry, I'm such a buzz kill."

I jumped up and turned the switches on, returning immediately to my spot next to him on the bed.

"You're not a buzz kill. Relax." He put his hands on my waist and turned me to face him. I took a deep breath, forcing myself to unwind.

Brady ran a hand beneath my white blouse, his fingers grazing across my stomach.

"I'll never get past the high of being your first," he said. "My cock is the only one that's ever gotten you off. I'd love to own your ass that same way."

My breathing got a little faster as I watched his lips, willing him to continue. He took his hand out from under my shirt and unfastened the top button, working the others one at a time.

"I want you to ride my cock while I give your ass a good fucking with my fingers," he said in a raspy tone. "I'll break that ass in and make you come so hard, Palmer."

He opened my shirt and stared at my breasts, his breath coming faster now, too.

"You can start Friday night," I said, my voice shaking with desire.

"I won't want to stop until I've come in your ass. Not Friday night, but once you let me start, I'll want to keep going further."

"I'll want that, too. I want to be at your mercy, Brady."

He groaned with satisfaction and slid the shirt from my shoulders, unhooking my bra and sliding it away next.

"I don't think it's mercy you want," he said, stroking his bulge as he stared at my exposed breasts. "I think you want me to use you for my own satisfaction."

"Yes, that's exactly what I want."

"You are so fucking sexy, Palmer."

I smiled, feeling that way as he eyed me. "Have you done anal with other women?"

"Yeah, but not like this. I'd had sex before you, but I was never the same after I made love to you."

"I need this, Brady. I need this escape. I want it so bad."

He stood and unbuttoned his pants. "Lay down."

As soon as I did, he unfastened my pants and pulled them off, taking my panties next. He spread my legs and forced my knees back, bending down and running his tongue over my clit. I was so turned on that it made me shudder.

"God, no," I said, writhing. "I'll come. I want you inside me."

"Not 'til Friday night." He circled my clit with his tongue then, and my arousal won out. I locked my legs around his face as I came hard, panting his name.

Never had I seen myself here. I was in a state of deep sadness, and my only escape was the warmth and sensation that only Brady could give me. I wondered where I'd be if we hadn't been paired on Derek and Adriane's house. I couldn't imagine. Now that he was back in my life, I couldn't imagine ever being without him again.

Chapter 15

Brady

Derek was taking his time looking around his great room, nodding appraisingly but saying nothing. We'd been busting ass all week to be ready for his inspection.

"This room is bigger than the house I grew up in," he said, shaking his head.

"I remember."

"It's incredible. Even better than I imagined. This fireplace ..." He gestured at the room's focal point, which rose two stories and was finished with slate in contrasting colors.

"You like it?"

"I love it."

"You'd better, asshole. I spent hours up on scaffolding laying the stone myself."

He clapped me on the shoulder, his expression hopeful. "This is where Adri and I will have our family. Not yet, but you know ... in a couple of years. She wanted a room where we can put up a huge Christmas tree and hang stockings. This room is it. It's perfect."

His words made me nod in agreement. I wanted that, too, but not with anyone but Palmer. And I figured her feelings about not being able to handle kids and Danny hadn't changed.

"Hey, you busy tonight?" Derek asked, interrupting my train of thought. "You wanna hang out?"

I shook my head. "I've got plans with Palmer."

"Palmer? You guys are seeing each other again, then?"

"Yeah."

He gave me an expectant look as the silence stretched. "And?"

"And what?"

"That's all you've got to say about it?"

I shrugged. "We're seeing each other and it's good. Her mom's close to the end, so that's pretty rough."

"You're there for her, though. That's the most important thing."

"I should've been there all along. I don't know how she's had the strength to do what she's done for the past year."

Derek's brow furrowed like he'd just thought of something. "What happens when you're done here? You goin' back to Denver?"

I sighed and ran a hand through my hair. "I don't know. I can't ask Palmer about the future because this isn't the time. I'm here for as long as she wants me to be."

"Adri's gonna be stoked about this," Derek said, grinning. "She really likes Palmer."

"Well, things are a little behind schedule with the design, so hopefully you guys will overlook that."

"Absolutely. No, we don't want her working on the house when her mom's this bad. You, either. You can shut down if you need to."

I nodded my appreciation. "Thanks, but my guys can keep things in the air here. I do need to get going now, though."

"Sure thing. Tell Palmer we're thinking of her. Let me know if there's anything you guys need."

"Thanks, D."

I headed for the trailer where I was meeting Hunter so he could drop me off at the car rental place. Hopefully they had full size pickups, because I wasn't driving a car.

Thoughts about vehicles were soon overridden by plans for tonight. I couldn't wait to live out Palmer's fantasy. Not only was it sexually exciting, she was trusting me to put her in a vulnerable position. I'd been apprehensive about doing anything that would hurt her at first, but the more I thought about it, the more charged up I got. If she wanted rough sex, why not? I wanted it, too.

Things between us were more honest this time around. More raw. She'd told me how much she wanted to be tied up and taken advantage of, which she never would have said the first time around. And even though I hadn't said it in so many words, the idea of exerting control over her excited me. She controlled my heart and soul. Sex was the only time I had the upper hand. She wanted to be controlled by me? She didn't even know it was something I'd been craving since kissing her in Derek's basement. Tonight would be a fantasy come true for both of us.

Palmer

We ate the chicken parmesan I'd made in relative silence, making small talk but mostly just looking at each other with a hunger that had nothing to do with food.

I ran dishwater, so preoccupied with thoughts of Brady that I didn't notice how hot the water was until my fingers unconsciously pulled their way out of the stream.

Brady's arms wrapped around my waist from behind and I broke out in goose bumps. He smelled so damn good tonight. The faint hint of his woodsy cologne mingled well with the cedar scent I loved.

"Hey," he said in my ear. "Fuck the dishes. We can think about them later."

I turned and looked up to his face. His plain black t-shirt was an exact match for his hair and the stubble I'd imagined feeling on my thighs during dinner.

"Okay," I said. "So I guess we'll need ... rope? God, I feel so kinky."

Brady smiled and reached for the wine bottle on the counter, tipping it to refill my glass. "I brought bungee cords."

"Oh, good." I started sipping the wine, but found I needed a gulp instead. "Did you bring anything else?"

"I might've. You still sure about this? You look nervous."

I took another swallow of wine before setting the glass on the counter to pace myself.

"It's a good nervous. I'm excited."

"So am I." He ran his hands up and down my arms, which were bare. I hadn't changed out of the sleeveless dress I'd worn to work today. "You cold?"

I shook my head. "It's from you touching me."

He arched his brows with amusement. "Do you always break out in goose bumps when I touch you? My ego would've liked to know that sooner."

"No. It's ... anticipation, I think."

"Meet me in the bedroom," he said with a very un-Brady-like wink. "I'm gonna get my bag from the car. Don't undress yet."

I went to my bedroom and looked over my bed with fresh eyes. I'd scored a deal on the four poster queen an estate sale and made my own gauzy cream canopy for it. Brady and I had been together in this bed many times, but never like this.

He walked in and set a small canvas bag on the dresser. I waited for him to open it and get what he needed to tie me up, but instead he approached me and wrapped a hand around my waist, pulling me closer to him.

"I'd never hurt you in anger," he said, and I nodded. "When you say you want it to hurt, do you mean you just want to be fucked so you're sore tomorrow?

"No. Make me scream. Bite me. Don't hold back."

He eyed me with appraisal and amusement. "Where is this coming from, baby? I've never seen this side of you."

"I want to be so overwhelmed that nothing else can get in my head tonight. And it's very hot to know I can trust you to do that without crossing the line."

He slid the strap of my dress down my shoulder, and then did the same to the other one. His eyes stayed locked on mine as he reached to the back of the dress and unzipped it, sliding it down until it fell and pooled at my feet.

The air on my skin incited my desire for him. I reached for him, but he stopped my hands, moving them back to my sides. He unhooked my strapless bra and it dropped to the floor silently. A breath slid slowly from my lips as he leaned into my neck and kissed me, the scrape of his scruff contrasting with the soft, warm touch of his mouth.

He kissed me just long enough to bring on an ache between my thighs. Then he bent to my breasts and took one nipple between his lips, sucking and licking until I moaned. I wanted more, and he gave it, sucking harder and cupping my ass with one of his big hands.

When his teeth closed around my nipple, my moan became a cry. He read it well, sinking his teeth in harder. It stung in a delicious way I felt in every nerve ending. When he released his hold, he soothed my throbbing nipple with a gentle lick.

My thighs trembled with anticipation when I felt his warm breath on my other nipple.

"Yes," I whispered. "Hurt me."

Both his hands sank into my ass this time, squeezing it hard while he sucked and bit my other nipple. I was about to say screw being tied up and beg him to fuck me now when he backed away and reached inside the bag, withdrawing several red nylon bungee cords.

"Panties off," he said, his eyes dark with something I'd never seen. Lust and maybe even a little anger. I dropped my panties and he laid a palm to my chest, kissing me soft and fast before pushing me to the bed.

I closed my eyes as he secured my wrists to the bedposts, his gentle touch reminding me that Brady would only hurt me in the ways I wanted him to. In a matter of minutes, I was his willing prisoner.

"All mine for tonight," he said in a low tone, his eyes roaming up and down my body.

"When have I not been all yours?" I challenged.

He arched his brows in surprise. "Since you decided not to marry me."

"I wanted to *wait*. Just wait. And you flipped out and left. And fucked other women."

Brady put a knee on the bed between my open legs, leaning over me. "I never loved any of them. It was just sex. You're the only one I've ever loved."

I met his eyes. "I still hate it. The thought of you fucking another woman makes me sick."

"Why?"

"Because you're mine."

His eyes closed for a second and then his lips were back on one of my nipples, teasing and sucking and biting.

He reached for something I couldn't see, even when I craned my neck to get a look.

"You like finding the line between pleasure and pain, Palmer?" he said, his fingers brushing over my exposed ass. "So do I."

I threw my head back, my body bucking with tension as his fingers circled me … there. No one had ever touched me there. Every muscle in my body tightened with resistance. His fingers were wet and warm, and when he lowered his lips to my neck and kissed me, I relaxed against his touch.

"Good girl," he murmured into my neck. A single fingertip eased its way in, and I surprised myself by moaning with pleasure. It wasn't just the forbidden fantasy of this that turned me on – it actually felt good.

"I like it," I said softly, moving my hips in time with his finger.

"You want more already?" he asked, his breath tickling my ear. "Pull your knees up as far as you can."

He'd left me a little slack, and I followed his instructions, exposing myself to him.

I moaned my approval as he slid two fingers in, circling my clit with his thumb. The pain was offset by the build of an orgasm.

"God*damn*, Palmer," Brady said, his erection stiff against my thigh. "I love being the first man to finger this sweet ass."

"Oh, my God," I cried. "Brady. Like that."

He got up on one knee beside me, his fingers continuing their delicious assault. When his hand wrapped gently around my throat, I gasped with surprise and met his eyes.

"Shh," he murmured softly. "Trust me."

He held my throat as his fingers worked me faster and harder. I pulled on the restraints, desperate to free myself from this vulnerable position but overcome with need for it at the same time.

It was like nothing I'd ever felt. I came so hard I saw stars, my vision clouding as a muffled scream escaped my throat. My body hung on to the high for several mindblowing seconds, and Brady relaxed his hold on my neck just as I started to slide back down to Earth.

"Holy shit!" I cried, gasping. "Brady ... I can't even ..."

He slid his fingers out of my ass, his thumb still slowly stroking me, and I circled my hips against him.

I was panting and trying to talk at the same time. "That was an out of body experience. I ... I've never felt anything like that."

I saw his satisfied smile for just a second before he leaned down to kiss my lips. "Glad you liked it."

"That throat thing. Is that why I came so hard? Have you ever done that to another woman? Be honest. No, don't."

"Yeah, it adds to sexual satisfaction. And no, I've never done in with anyone else. I'm being honest."

"Has anyone done it to you?"

"No."

I met his eyes hopefully. "Can I?"

"You want to do that to me?" he asked, amused. "With those delicate little hands?"

"I'm stronger than I look."

"You can do anything you want to me and I'll love it." He flicked his tongue over my nipple, bringing it to attention. "Another night."

His mouth roamed every inch of my body. And it wasn't the usual spots that set me on fire. The time he spent kissing my hips and calves and shoulders left me panting once again. Those spots had never been lavished with attention.

It felt so good, and guilt about my mom being sick in bed while I was here crept in.

"Please, Brady," I begged. "Make everything else go away. I don't care if it hurts, just make me forget the pain inside."

His eyes searched mine for a couple long seconds before he looked away.

"I can't."

"Yes – I want it."

He shook his head and gave me a look of apology. "Part of me – a very sick part – gets off on the idea of hurting you because you hurt me. But I can't do it."

"But—"

"I can't make the pain of your mom go away, Palmer. Or, if I can, I shouldn't. I hate like hell that you have to feel it, but you do. I'm here, though. You can cry or scream or beat the shit out of me if it'll help. Just let go."

Tears welled in my eyes as he spoke. "Will you stay until … until she's gone?" I asked hoarsely. "Please?"

"Yes. I'm not leaving."

"I want you, Brady. Right now."

He pulled his clothes off in a matter of seconds, meeting my eyes as he pulled a square package from the pocket of his jeans on the floor.

I shook my head. No condom. Not this time. I'd stayed on the pill for some unknown reason that now made complete sense.

His eyes softened as he dropped the package to the floor. He climbed over me, kissed my lips softly and then thrust his hips against mine, burying every inch of himself deep inside me. He'd never gone all the way in on the first stroke before, and I cried out loudly and arched my body against his. Was I crying from the pain or the pleasure? I didn't know and I didn't care.

I waited for him to draw back and pound back into me, but he was completely still. My core quivered with anticipation.

"Brady," I said, his name coming out in a whimper. "Please. Please, don't stop."

But he remained motionless, his green eyes studying me. "I'm not moving until you tell me something," he said softly.

"What?" I would have told him anything in this moment, for an end to this sweet agony.

I rocked my hips into his, sighing with pleasure from the contact. He moved an arm between us, his forearm pinning my hips to the bed. I cried out with frustration, desperate for release.

Being completely at his mercy was an erotic thrill like I'd never imagined. I couldn't move, but there was no fear. I trusted Brady with my life. He was giving me what I'd asked for – his complete control over my body. But it was torturous, having him buried inside me while motionless.

"What do you want me to tell you?" I asked, desperation in my tone.

His lips hovered just over mine, his warm breath adding to my frantic desire. I let my tongue reach for his lips, the tip just reaching his bottom one.

"Tell me something that's true," he said in a low, sexy rumble.

"Uh ...I think I'm gonna come if you move even an inch," I said, panting and making a futile effort to arch my hips toward his. "That's true."

He pulled his face back and his lips curled into a smile.

"No. What I mean is ... I wish like hell I would've fought for you. For what we had. Not let my stupid pride rule me. That's the truth, Palmer."

His bright eyes flickered with emotion, and I wanted so badly to reach up and stroke his cheek.

"You're the only man I've ever wanted," I said, keeping my eyes locked on his.

He leaned his face to mine and brushed a kiss across my lips. "I didn't believe you at first when you said you'd never sucked anyone's cock when we were first together. You were way too good at it."

My lips parted in shock. "Brady. I swear."

He smiled, grinding his hips against mine. I gave a vocal sigh of pleasure. "It's true, baby. Tell me something true."

"I wear my engagement ring to bed every night because it makes me feel close to you," I said, averting his gaze.

"This whole time?"

I nodded silently. Brady pulled several inches out of me, rewarding my honesty with a deep thrust back in.

"I realize now that it was never about money," he said, remorse in his voice.

"I want to touch you so bad right now," I said pleadingly.

His eyes twinkled and he smiled. "You can do better than that, baby. Talk to me."

He dropped his face to my neck, where he kissed me softly, all the way up to my jaw line.

"Okay," I said, reveling in the feel of his mouth on my skin. "Last night I fantasized about you taking me to a big, open field of flowers. You undressed me and just looked at me like ... like you used to do. Then you laid me down and put my feet on your shoulders and gave me mind blowing oral sex."

"Sex in the outdoors, huh?" he said, grinning widely. "We can do that."

He pulled his hips back, shoving himself in with a punishing thrust.

"Yes," I cried, biting my lip as the tremble of an orgasm started in me. When he moved again, I looked into his eyes, wanting to tell him one last truth. "I need you, Brady. I need you. Not just for my body — for my soul."

His face twisted with his effort to hold back and he slid his arm out from under my hips. I arched into him, my entire body gripped with the electricity of the orgasm that was seizing me.

"I'm still in love with you," Brady said, ramming himself into me with brute force. "I've always been in love with you."

We came together in an explosion of screams and groans. When Brady seized and emptied himself into me, I felt our spiritual connection once again. We'd exposed our truths to each other, and there was no going back.

But I didn't want to go back. I wanted this moment with my best friend, lover and partner to be just one of many more.

"I'm still in love with you, too," I said. "And I still really want to touch you."

With a grin, he reached up and unfastened the ties on my wrists and then my ankles. When they fell away, I wrapped my arms and legs around him, unable to stop myself from crying against his chest.

"I don't want to be without you ever again," Brady said, his big hand stroking over my hair and down my back.

"No. Me either," I said. "Danny and I will move, after my mom …"

I couldn't say the word, my voice breaking just from the thought.

"Shh," Brady said, pulling me against him tightly. "I'm here now, and I'm not leaving you. The rest'll work itself out."

My tension drained away with his reassurance. I was safe in his arms, and exhaustion quickly pulled me into a deep sleep.

Chapter 16

Palmer

I pushed Mom's bedroom door open, forcing a smile.

"Hey, Julie's here," I said. "From hospice. She's going to make you more comfortable."

Mom gave a single nod and sighed. "It's been a hard day."

"The patch doesn't seem to help much anymore," Amanda explained to Julie from the other side of Mom's bed.

The nurse set down her bag of supplies and reached for Mom's hand, squeezing it.

"I'm going to increase your dose and also give you some medicine that will dissolve on your tongue," she said. "It'll help."

"She hasn't been eating or drinking," I said, folding my arms across myself protectively. "Will you tell her she has to eat and drink to keep her strength?"

Julie, a redhead with a snowy white complexion, glanced at me and smiled. "It's okay if she doesn't want to. We don't want to force that."

She opened a package and moved to put something in Mom's mouth, but Mom held up a hand to stop her.

"Palmer," she said weakly. "I need you to listen to me."

"Of course, Mom." I took her hand and sat down in my chair next to her bed, leaning close to keep her from having to talk very loud.

"I'm sorry I prioritized Danny over you every time. I could have gotten help with him – I should've."

Julie and Amanda both headed for the door to give us privacy. I wished they'd stay, because I did not want to have this conversation with Mom. I felt like I was suffocating.

"Mom, no," I said. "You don't have to do this."

A hand squeezed my shoulder from behind and I turned. It was Amanda.

"Let her," she said softly. "It's important to her."

Reluctantly, I nodded and turned back to Mom.

"I'm sorry for cutting you off," I said.

"It's okay," she said, wincing. I knew she was in pain right now, and delaying her relief for this conversation. "I know you're trying to protect me. But don't. I should've given you more."

"There were times when I felt that way growing up," I admitted. "But I always knew you loved me and Danny the same. I knew that, Mom."

Her eyes sparkled, a contrast to her sunken cheeks. "I do. I love you both so much." She ran her tiny thumb over my fingers, sighing softly. "I was hoping you'd have the ring back on. I love Brady, too, you know."

"I love him too," I said, a tear sliding down my face. "I'm not letting him go again."

"Be happy."

"I promise," I said, wiping my cheeks with the back of my hand. "And I promise I'll take care of Danny. Always."

"I know," she said, a smile curling up the corners of her lips. "But not all alone, Palmer. Not all alone, okay?"

"Not alone," I promised. "I love you so much, Mom. So does Danny."

She smiled wide, her eyes glistening before they fluttered shut. But I knew she wasn't sleeping. She was trying to cope with the tremendous pain she was in. I went to the door and asked Julie to come back in.

While she administered medication to Mom, I stood outside the door with Amanda, my back to the wall.

"Thanks," I whispered, another tear escaping.

Brady was craning his neck from the couch, where he sat with Danny. I could tell he was trying to figure out from my expression whether I needed him to comfort me. Just that was comforting.

"She's close to the end, isn't she?" I said, my voice catching. "And she knows."

"People seem to have a sense about it."

I sighed deeply, studying Amanda's pale blue eyes.

"It's hard to see her in pain," I said.

She nodded with understanding. "That can be controlled. She can basically be kept in a state of sleep until the end."

"And she won't hurt?"

"She won't hurt. I've seen a lot of people go that way at the nursing home and it's very peaceful."

Brady approached, wrapping an arm around my shoulders. I leaned against him, sadness overtaking me as I realized I'd probably just had the last conversation I'd ever have with my Mom.

Brady

Danny surveyed the bright green grass of Wrigley Field, awestruck.

"Cubs!" he cried, pointing to the dugout.

"Yeah. The game starts soon, are you ready?"

His expression told me he'd been ready for this his whole life. I didn't think he fully grasped that this was the place we saw on TV, but he knew something good was about to go down.

I parked his chair in a prime spot in the suite where Derek was meeting us, wishing I'd thought of this idea sooner. Danny was more quiet than usual at home. He hadn't seen his mom in more than a week, but he'd stopped asking about her.

Palmer struggled over whether she should bring him in to see their mother. But she always decided to respect her mom's wish and leave it this way. Janelle knew her son would be scared by seeing her in her current condition.

I was helping Danny sip the lemonade a waiter had delivered to our suite when Derek walked in, clapping me on the shoulder.

"Hey, man," he said. "This must be Danny."

"Yeah. Danny, this is my friend Derek."

Danny gave him a wave, grinning and gesturing toward the field.

"Cubs," he said. "Play baseball."

"We'll fix you up with a jersey and a ball," Derek said. "I'm really glad to meet you."

Danny became engrossed in the big screen monitor that was visible from our suite. Derek and I couldn't compete with the sights and sounds of the stadium.

"How's Palmer?" Derek asked.

I shrugged. "Pretty upset, but hanging in there. It's hard."

"Are you guys back together?"

"Yeah. We've worked a lot of things out. It's a lot more … real between us this time, if that makes sense."

"Sure it does. An untested love may not be what you think it is. But when you get through shit together, that makes things stronger."

"I don't care when we get married anymore," I said, staring out at the sea of faces in the stands. "I mean, I want to marry her. But what matters more than marrying her is loving her. It wasn't like that before. I just wanted to make her mine."

Derek arched his brows and nodded. "You've come a long way. I'm proud of you, man."

I gave him a dismissive grunt. "Let's not get all sappy."

"Seriously. I want you guys to get married and have a bunch of little dark, brooding Bradys."

I smiled. "I want that, too. She'll be an amazing mother."

"You'd better name the first one Derek."

"Yeah, we'll have lots of time to think on that. We've got a lot in front of us still, with her mom and getting one of the houses fixed up and sold."

"You guys moving in together?"

"I hope so," I said, nodding. "Haven't asked her yet, though. It's not the right time."

Talking about Palmer made me think of her. I wanted to be with her right now, but was trying to help by taking care of Danny so she wouldn't worry about him. I texted her.

Me: Danny's having a good time. How r u?

Palmer: Okay. Mom's sleeping. Thanks again for taking him.

I pictured her sitting in the darkened bedroom, alone with her mom. But then I remembered that Amanda was there. Still, I wished it was me next to her.

Me: Miss u and love u.

Palmer: Me too. So much.

This was what I needed. Not a wedding date or a marriage certificate. She finally needed me back. I'd be the man she could count on, not just now, but forever.

Palmer

The soothing melody of Sarah McLachlan's voice was the only sound in the room. Mom had always loved this CD, and I'd chosen it immediately when Julie suggested music.

Danny was staying at Amanda's apartment at her request. Mom had been in a perpetual state of sleep for two full days. Julie had been here for the past twenty-four hours. Everyone seemed to know the time was close.

But knowing and accepting are very different things. I sat at Mom's side, holding her hand and watching her chest rise and fall. I willed her next breath each time her chest dropped with an exhale.

The gurgling sound didn't mean she was in pain. I reminded myself of that as I waited. Seven … eight … nine – nearly ten seconds before she inhaled again.

This was natural, Julie had assured me, but still – brutal to witness.

I twisted my hand in Mom's, brushing her fingers over my platinum engagement ring.

"I'm wearing it," I whispered. "Brady asked me to put it back on, and I said yes. And when we get married, I know you'll be watching."

Brady rubbed my shoulders reassuringly. He'd been standing behind me for hours, not saying a word.

"I love you, Mom," I said. "This is the time when I'm supposed to be telling you the things I never said and should have. But I'm really glad I already said them. And you did, too."

I hadn't been counting, but I knew she'd gone a long time between breaths there. I rubbed her hand and her arm. I brushed the hair from her forehead and kissed it, a tear falling from my cheek onto hers.

Julie sat on the other side of the bed, ready to administer more medication if needed. Uncle Jay had come this morning to say goodbye to his only sister, but he was too overcome with emotion to stay until the end. I assured him he'd been here for her when it mattered.

Part of me wished Danny could be here, but I knew it would scare him and upset him. Amanda was talking to him today about Heaven, which we'd brought up with him last week.

It was me, Brady and Julie, and it was an oddly tranquil moment when I waited for her chest to rise that last time and … it didn't.

I cried quietly as Julie pressed a stethoscope to Mom's chest. Brady wrapped his arms around me from behind, holding me tight as we waited.

"She's gone," Julie finally said.

I let out a loud sob, turning to wrap my arms around Brady and bury my face in his chest. It wasn't just for her death that I cried, but for the year-long ordeal she'd been through. Treatments, hair loss, fatigue, vomiting, and the knowledge that soon the tumors in her lungs and brain would kill her.

Cancer had killed my mother, but it hadn't taken her life. Her life had been spent loving and living. And I fully believed she'd faced the end on her terms; making peace before moving on.

Brady

The cool breeze that blew through the tall trees on the cemetery's perimeter carried a promise of fall. The sunny, cloudless sky didn't feel right today. The day we laid Janelle to rest should have been dark and rainy.

Palmer clutched my hand as the pastor finished his remarks. Her hazel eyes were a swirl of green and brown today. I sensed a newfound peace in her.

At the end of the service, she kissed her fingers and pressed them to the dark wood casket we'd chosen for her mother. She'd let me cover the cost of the best service money could buy. Janelle deserved every exotic flower and more.

"I love you," Palmer whispered to the casket, wiping away a tear before turning to me.

I hated to let go of her hand, but I had to so I could push Danny's chair through the grassy turf of the cemetery. Just as I reached for the handles to push it, another set of hands landed there.

"I've got it," Troy said.

"Hey." My chest tightened with emotion as I looked him over, clean-shaven and wearing a dark, well-fitted suit. "I didn't see you here."

He nodded and reached out to hug Palmer before taking over with Danny's chair. Palmer and I followed, reaching the limo just as Amanda did.

"Who are you?" she demanded, looking from Danny to Troy. Her defensive tone made me smile. This girl really loved Danny.

My brother paused, looking dumbstruck before he finally answered. "I'm Troy. Brady's brother."

"Oh." She looked down at her dark shoes. "Sorry."

Palmer looked like she wanted to smile. "Where's your mom?" she asked, looking around. "Isn't she riding with us?"

"No, she's meeting us at the restaurant," I said.

"Okay, just the five of us, then."

"No, I don't ... I shouldn't ride with the family," Amanda said, taking a step back. "I just wanted to check on Danny."

Palmer put an arm around Amanda, finally letting the smile come out. "Of course you're riding with us. You *are* family."

And it was true. As hard as her mother's death had been, it pulled us all closer together. Whether or not we'd said our wedding vows, Palmer and Danny were my family. And Amanda, Georges and Troy were part of our untraditionally perfect unit.

Palmer and I had paid a price for our mistakes, but we'd learned from them. We'd also learned from the mistakes of others. After her final conversation with her mom, she'd started saying something I couldn't get out of my head.

I took her hand in mine, making a promise of those words — not just to her and Danny, but to myself.

Never alone.

Seven months later

Palmer

I lugged my oversize bag of fabric and wood samples through the door of the house, marveling as I always did at the open, vaulted ceilings. Skylights dominated the ceiling, allowing in filtered sunlight. But my favorite feature in this home was the wood planks that made up the rest of the ceiling. Their fresh scent reminded me of Brady.

"Hey," he said, reaching for the bag on my shoulder. He was hanging trim – I could tell from the tiny wood shavings that spotted his dark hair. After he slung the bag over his shoulder, he leaned down and kissed me. I pressed my hands to his cheeks and went back in for a longer kiss.

"This place is looking gorgeous," I said, admiring it when we parted.

Its location had special meaning to me, too. Grant Brothers Builders was developing a house deep in the wooded lot Brady and I had snuck away to for lunchtime interludes while building Derek and Adriane's house.

"I've got hardwood samples I need you to look at and decide on," Brady said, taking my hand and walking me to the wall of windows in the great room that looked out into the forest.

Brady had only cleared what he had to for the footprint of the house. The trees that nestled all around it gave it a lush, treehouse feeling.

"I think we should let the buyers choose the floors," I said. Much as I wanted him to cover the entire place in wide planks of Brazilian Cherry, that choice might not suit everyone.

"Nah … you choose. You're a designer. It'll have more pop to potential buyers with flooring."

I walked over to the samples he'd arranged in rows in the home's open future kitchen.

"They're all so beautiful," I said. "The Brazilian Cherry reminds me of the living room floor at Mom's house. I see some of the same tones in it. She loved that floor."

"So that one?"

I sighed and folded my arms across my chest. "Brady, this is someone else's house, so my personal attachment to that floor shouldn't be a factor. I'm telling you, we need to let the buyers choose it."

"The house will be sold finished. We talked about that from the beginning."

I nodded. "And when Georges and I first partnered with you on this, that sounded like so much fun to me. I loved choosing all the finishes at Derek and Adriane's house. But we've got prospective buyers who want to be involved in the big choices, like flooring and cabinets."

Brady scowled at me. "What prospective buyers? This house isn't even on the market yet."

"Well, Georges has been spreading the word to some of our clients."

"No. I'm not doin' that. I'm not having him drag people through this house while we're working on it."

I approached and rubbed his forearms. "But if we can sell it, we won't have to pay a real estate commission. That's better for the bottom line."

"I told you, my bottom line is excellent. You don't need to worry about that."

"Well, Sinclair Brammer's bottom line isn't so great," I said. Georges and I were in the black, but we wanted to be careful so we could stay that way.

Brady cupped my cheeks in his massive, work-worn palms. "I'm paying you guys a flat fee for this. You don't have to worry about the money. I'll pay you more if you need me to."

"No. It's just ... I'm sorry, I know you're the contractor, but ..."

One corner of his mouth quirked up in a grin. "Go on. Second guess me. I know you want to."

"It's not that I want to. But some of the decisions you made on this design aren't going to be for every buyer. The ramps, instead of stairs?"

He shrugged. "It's a better design aesthetic. And it's a smart move, given the number of Baby Boomers on the market."

"I agree, and it is pretty. But the elevator from the garage all the way up to the second level?"

"It's a wheelchair-accessible home. You and I both know how important that is."

I nodded, trying to think of the most diplomatic way to get my point across. "But it adds a lot to the cost, and the buyers may not even want it. I love you, but I'm seriously starting to wonder how you make so much money when you make such ... odd decisions."

He threw his head back and laughed, sliding one hand from my cheek around to the back of my neck.

"Baby, we decided this would be our fun project. You know, after your mom passed, we wanted a little bit of a break from things. This house allowed us to work together and do it at a pace that gave us plenty of time with Danny."

I ran my hands over the hard, defined muscles of his back. "I know, and I've loved it. I really have. Working with your business to design new builds is literally saving my business. I just don't want you losing so much money just so I can have fun. I'm in a better place now. Let's start thinking of this house from a business perspective."

He nodded. "Okay. But I'm still the general contractor, and I say we're selling it finished. So pick out the flooring."

I backed up, my heart rate picking up with aggravation. "I hate it when you do that."

"What?"

"Placate me. Act like you've given me something when really you haven't."

He rubbed a hand over his dark, unshaven jaw line. "Palmer. Will you just pick out the flooring?"

I folded my arms across my chest. "No. We need to be showing this house to prospective buyers. And when we sell it, if they choose Brazilian Cherry, I'll stand corrected."

He groaned and rolled his eyes skyward. "I don't want the house shown yet."

"Why did you say we were partnering on this project if I'm just here to choose paint colors and flooring?"

"You've done a lot more than that," he said, giving me a pointed look. "I'm gonna put in the Brazilian Cherry."

I pursed my lips, feeling a glare coming on. "But that's one of the most expensive floors on the market and this is a 4,500 square-foot house. Please, think about the cost."

"You wanna see my bank statements?" he challenged. "I told you, the cost doesn't matter."

"Fine, have it your way." I turned to leave, but my angry stomp wasn't as fast as he was.

"Hey." He put a hand on my hip and turned me to face him. "This house is for us. It was supposed to be a surprise."

My anger slid away in an instant, replaced by disbelief.

"What? Are you …? For us?"

He nodded, a glint of hopeful happiness in his bright green eyes. "We're already living together. And since we're getting married in two months, I thought … this would be a good wedding present."

My eyes filled with tears as I looked around the huge, beautiful home with fresh eyes. "It's for Danny. The ramps and the elevator."

"Yeah. Even though he might be moving into the group home, we'll want him here every weekend. And … you know. Who knows what the future holds? We could always move him back in with us and our home will be ready."

I flung myself at him, pressing my body against his as I squeezed him as hard as my arms would allow.

"I love you. You're so incredible."

I cried against his chest, overwhelmed with emotion. This home was four times as big as my tiny two bedroom bungalow and ten times nicer, but that wasn't what brought this on. Brady was completely invested in our little family. His devotion to me and Danny had never wavered.

"I love you, too," he said, pressing his cheek to the top of my head. "So you like it? It's not too far out of the city for you?"

I shook my head and wiped my cheeks. "It's perfect. Danny will love it."

"I've come close to telling you so many times. It's kind of a relief that you know now."

I looked up at the open loft bedroom, which Brady still needed to put up the railing for. "That's our bedroom?"

"Yep. I found some railing with glass panels for there and the staircase. I don't want any openings because, you know ... kids, maybe, someday."

He gave me a hopeful glance that melted my heart. "I definitely want that," I said. My cheeks warmed as I remembered something and laughed.

"What?" he asked.

"I was just thinking about when we ... you know, christened the house that one time up against the wall in the bathroom ... I just like knowing it was *our* house."

"Lots more rooms to christen," he said, his gaze raking me from head to toe. "We could start with our future bedroom."

I put my arms around his neck, wrapping my legs around his waist when he cupped his hands around my ass to pick me up.

"We could," I said against his lips. "In fact, I think we *should*."

Epilogue

Four years later

Palmer

My brother's deep, carefree laugh had always been my favorite sound in the world, but now I had a new one. I never tired of hearing his laughter mingled with my daughter's two-year-old giggles of amusement.

"Uncle Danny!" Elle shrieked, laughing as her fat little legs carried her away from him. "Chase me!"

And he did, wheeling himself after her around the open circle of our great room, entryway and kitchen for at least the fifteenth time. This had been their favorite game since before Elle could walk. She'd crawl, squealing with delight when he followed.

Brady's mom was watching from the kitchen island, smiling at her granddaughter. With tiny black pigtails and bright green eyes, Elle had both her grandparents wrapped around her little finger.

"Should I wait to make lunch?" my mother-in-law asked, furrowing her brow. She was already busy preparing for our annual Thanksgiving meal tomorrow, and I thought Brady and Tucker should make do with leftovers from the fridge when they returned. But this was what Marie loved to do – take care of her men.

I was about to answer when Brady opened the door, his wide grin making my heart pick up speed. He'd bundled in lined canvas work clothes for this brisk winter outing with his father, and his rugged look made me want to sneak away with him and warm away the ruddy chill on his cheeks.

"It's our best yet," he said proudly. Danny and Elle came to watch as Brady and Tucker hauled in the giant Christmas tree they'd cut down in the woods.

"That Rockefeller tree's got nothing on this one," Tucker said, straining under the weight of the massive tree.

The vaulted ceilings in our home allowed us to put up a ridiculously large Christmas tree every year, and we seemed to be having a contest to make each one taller than the last.

"That's beautiful," I murmured, approaching them. "Can I help?"

Brady gave me a look of caution as I approached and I stopped, laying a hand over my stomach. I was just finishing my first trimester of pregnancy with our second baby, and he was taking care of me the same way he had with Elle. That meant no lifting anything, no housework and lots of backrubs.

I was happily soaking it all in. Until this week, I'd been exhausted and sick with this pregnancy. It was one of the reasons Tucker and Marie were staying with us right now – to help with Danny and Elle.

Brady and Tucker shed their coats and set to getting the tree upright.

"Daddy!" Elle cried, tugging on his jeans. "Tree! Look at the tree!"

He swept her into his arms for a closer look. "You like it, princess?"

She wrapped her arms around his neck and squealed. "Yes!"

"What do you think, Danny?" Marie asked, putting an arm around his shoulders.

"Good," he said, staring at the tree with an awestruck expression.

The word filled me with warmth from head to toe. It was how I felt right now. Life was so good. I had a pang of longing for my mom. She would have been in love with the granddaughter who'd been named after her. My business was going well, and Brady's was going exceptionally well. We had the means to give Mom the help she deserved so she could enjoy her family.

But that wasn't meant to be. I hoped she could see us right now, though. Seeing Danny and me surrounded by our family would've made her so happy.

Tree upright at last, Brady came over and wrapped his arms around me, pulling me against him. His shirt was damp with sweat and his woodsy scent was stronger than usual after his bout with a fifteen-foot tall pine.

"Like it?" he asked me softly.

"I love it." I sighed happily. "Will you build a fire and sit on the couch with me?"

"I'll get the fire," Tucker said, smiling at us as he glanced over. He'd rebuilt his business and more importantly, his relationships with his family after his release from prison. But I still sensed that he took none of this for granted.

As Brady sat down on our large leather sofa and pulled me into his lap, I had the same sense myself. Life was fragile. And my year apart from Brady had shown me how hard it could be to navigate it alone.

I felt myself drifting into a warm, blissful sleep in Brady's arms, lulled by the rise and fall of his chest. How had I ever convinced myself I didn't need this? He was the other half of my heart. Life would bring us ups and downs, but together, we'd get through them and come out stronger on the other side.

Author's Note

Thank you so much for reading Unspoken. If you enjoyed it, I'd sincerely appreciate a review at the site of the retailer you purchased it from. Please connect with me on Facebook, Twitter and/or Goodreads to stay up on all my news and releases. You can also sign up for my newsletter, see trailers for my books and access other exclusive information at my website. I LOVE messages from my readers, so drop me a line anytime!

Acknowledgements

While all my books have a small piece of me in them, Unspoken is especially personal. I lost my dad to cancer four years ago. I drew on that experience for this book, and I hope it resonates with others who have lost a parent. It's a loss like no other; one I don't think anyone is ever completely prepared for.

My village is growing, and I'm so thankful for that. My first thanks have to go to my friend and fellow author Stephanie Reid. I went through a developmental struggle with this book and her help was invaluable. She's so much more than just a talented writer and I encourage you to check out her work if you like mine.

Carrie Jones, beta reader-extraordinaire, helped with research for this book. Her medical perspective was invaluable.

My assistant, Pam Million, was there for me in so many ways. She is always up to read a few pages or an entire book if I need her to. She's always honest and is a friend I can always rely on. I probably could write a book without her and her Power Ranger stickers, but I don't want to.

Denise Milano Sprung's support, encouragement and feedback helped make this book what it is. It's an honor to pledge a portion of the release week sales for this book to the Keith Milano Memorial Fund, which Denise formed to honor her brother. It's impossible to quantify how many people have been helped or saved by her efforts to advocate for the mentally ill, which makes the work all the more valuable.

Chatter PR helps with my promotions so I have more time for writing. Their enthusiasm for every aspect of my work means a lot to me.

Editor Gayle Evers made this book better with her developmental expertise. She's unfailingly patient with me and is also a top-notch line editor. I'm grateful she's in my corner.

Beta readers Michelle Tan, Chelle Northcutt, Katrina Kirkpatrick and Rosarita Reader helped make this book better. They are not just beta readers, but also dear friends.

Another friend, Karla Sorenson, is an unending source of encouragement and inspiration. I love our author support group.

My friends in Random Moon Books also give me encouragement, inspiration and friendship. I'm deeply grateful to be part of a group of women who are truly rooting for each other in every way.

If I could tackle hug 153 people at the same time, it would be the members of Rothert's Readers, my reader group. You all mean the world to me. Your enthusiasm keeps me going on a daily basis.

As always, the biggest thanks go to my husband and our three boys. I love you all so very much.